THE MAYAN TEMPLE

ORDER OF THE BLACK SUN - BOOK 30

PRESTON WILLIAM CHILD

❀ Created with Vellum

1

CHAPTER ONE – THE VANISHING

David Purdue hacked away at the thicket of vines surrounding him. No matter how much he managed to cut away with his machete, more and more tendrils slithered down to block his path. They wrapped around him, trying to entangle him but he refused to let himself be restrained. The only way to get out of such a mess was to press forward. So, Purdue would keep swinging his blade and keep walking forward until he was past all of the obstacles in his path.

His life had recently come across far more obstacles than the vines draped in front of him. He had lost everything. His greatest enemies, the shadowy Order of the Black Sun, had stripped him of his wealth, his prized collection of artifacts, and had even taken most of his closest allies hostage. But he refused to give in, and was slowly building himself back up—preparing to strike back at the secret society for trying to destroy everything that he was.

He wasn't sure if he was ready for war, but he would have to be. His opportunity to pull off a sneak attack against his unsuspecting enemies had passed him by. The Order of the Black Sun knew he was alive and they knew he was still acting against them. He had managed to survive their last few attempts to kill him but he knew how unyielding his enemies could be, and he knew how psychotic their leader was. Julian Corvus wouldn't stop coming for him, and now that Julian had gained immortality, he would never, ever stop. Purdue wouldn't be able to evade them forever, but Julian could make sure that the chase lasted forever.

He needed to end this feud and retake his life sooner rather than later. The Black Sun still had his friends, Nina, Jean, and Charles hostage.

Dr. Nina Gould was one of his closest friends, and he had been traveling the world with her for a long time now. They had a complicated relationship sometimes, but he cared about her more than most people.

Jean-Luc Gerard was one of his more recent colleagues, but he had made a good impression during their search for a powerful spell book. He was an occult expert based out of the French Quarter in New Orleans, and Purdue knew that if their partnership continued that Jean would be essential in helping him with any further supernatural artifacts that he may come across. It had always been a weak point in Purdue's skill set, but Jean was the perfect person to help balance it out. He knew more than Purdue probably ever could.

And lastly, Charles. He should never have even been taken prisoner. Since Nina and Jean had both actively helped Purdue collect artifacts, and Nina had been the one to nearly finish off Julian for good, it made sense that they would be taken hostage. But Charles was just Purdue's butler. Sure, he was a close confidant and an essential part of Purdue's life, but he had never participated in anything that could be seen as hostile toward the Black Sun. The most he had done was help try and protect the artifacts when the Black Sun came to take everything.

Now Nina, Charles, and Jean-Luc remained as the order's prisoners, but the fight had escalated, and Purdue knew Julian would want to use his hostages against him. If Julian hadn't killed them already, then they were in more danger than ever.

Unfortunately, Purdue's hopes of having a good amount of weapons to use hadn't come to pass like he hoped. He had only been able to collect two useful artifacts that he could actually wield in the coming battles. He had an old dead witch's book of shadows that was full of magics that he was too terrified to use. He had also found a pearl on the ocean floor that could control the seas. They were very powerful relics—but still wouldn't be enough. The Order of the Black Sun had a stockpile of artifacts they had collected, including a great number of which they had stolen from Purdue's private collection. He knew those items well and understood that combined with the Black Sun's own relics, he was severely outgunned.

He couldn't exactly match the Black Sun's numbers either. They had dozens, if not hundreds of operatives at their disposal. Purdue had about half a dozen allies left on a good day and the majority of those friends weren't looking to be drafted into a war that they had no real stake in. It didn't involve them, not really.

The only exception was Purdue's longtime colleague, Sam Cleave. He wanted to free Nina and finally put an end to the Order of the Black Sun just as much as Purdue did.

For some time, the Black Sun believed that he was dead—and he practically was. But that anonymity hadn't lasted forever. His enemies knew that he was alive now, and it was kill or be killed. The war was coming, and he had to be ready for it, and make sure that he had enough firepower to take on the order.

That need had brought him to the jungles of Honduras.

He had heard rumors about a very interesting place with remarkable power. That sounded like it had potential to be something useful to him, especially with his battle looming ahead of him. Any little discovery could make all the difference in the world.

The locals said that a strange temple had miraculously appeared deep in the heart of the jungle. It seemed a little hard to believe, but Purdue had seen plenty of things that were supposed to be just as improbable. Those spreading the rumors claimed that this temple appeared one night out of thin air. It was not built. When he asked if it was possible that no one had ever found it before and that this could all just have been a coincidence that no one had explored that area—they all said it would've been seen.

They were convinced that this temple was something new—but no building just appeared out of thin air, or grew out of the ground, or any of the number of ludicrous possibilities that were being thrown around by the locals.

Based on the amount of vines and overgrowth that he was tearing his way through, it couldn't have been that well-traversed of a place. It certainly wasn't a popular tourist destination, that much was obvious. And now, with that temple suddenly appearing, no one dared to go near it, petrified that it had come to somehow try to harm them.

Purdue wasn't spooked by it all. He was mostly intrigued.

Some people were so afraid of the unknown but Purdue was the kind of man that would dive headfirst into it. It was amazing what could be found in the most unexplored places that people never dared to tread.

Purdue swung his machete a few times, trying

to break through some branches in his way. When they snapped and dropped to the ground, the branches brought down a shroud of greenery with them. It was like a curtain opened up and Purdue was now staring at an enormous monolith—the temple that everyone was raving about.

"...the hell?"

The temple was old, and made of dark slabs of rock. It must have taken so many years to build, generations even. It stood at least four stories tall and was an imposing sight among all of the natural wonders around it.

Trees lay strewn about around the structure, having been completely uprooted from the earth. It was like a bomb had detonated in the middle of the jungle—or that an ancient temple had appeared out of thin air with such force that it decimated the wildlife around its entry point...but that didn't seem possible. Then again, he was already staring at something that was supposed to be impossible. The temple shouldn't have been there at all.

Purdue began walking toward the peculiar temple. He was very glad to be out of all of the webs of vines and branches that had made his hike a very challenging one. Now he just had to watch his step around all of the toppled trees between him and the temple.

"You there!"

Purdue nearly leaped out of his own skin at the sound. He wasn't expecting anyone to be so far out, especially not this close to the place that everyone was so petrified of. According to everyone he'd spoken to, no one would dare get as close as he was planning to get, but here someone was.

A bald man walked toward him with a red haired woman beside him. By the way they were dressed—with all of the excessive hiking gear—they looked like tourists. Maybe they were just exploring the mysterious haunted temple. But there was something unnerving about the way the bald man was looking at him, something behind the tightness of his expression.

"I'm sorry if we startled you."

There was no 'if' about it. He was more than a little startled by those bastards' presence.

"Not a problem," Purdue lied.

The woman peered at the machete in Purdue's hand. He didn't want to scare her so pointed the machete over to the tree line. "It wasn't an easy walk to get here. Had to cut my way through the forest." He then acknowledged the downed trees around their feet. "This...I didn't do obviously."

"Obviously," the bald man said, looking over to the temple. "You out here to look at this thing too?"

"I am," Purdue said.

"Fascinating, isn't it?" The bald man held out a hand to greet him. "I am Lucius. This is Charlotte."

Purdue offered a smile but didn't receive one in return. There was something off about those two, but he couldn't figure out exactly what. Maybe they were just terrible at meeting people.

"I'm David," Purdue offered in return.

"We know."

The thinnest of smiles barely graced Lucius' face, but suddenly his tightened expression seemed sharp.

"We were hoping to bump into you, Purdue. Ever since that temple appeared, we've hoped that you would have to come and see it yourself just like Corvus said you might."

Purdue took a step back and tightened his grip on the blade in his hands. These weren't any kind of tourists at all. They were members of the Order of the Black Sun.

"Like a fly in a spider's web. That's how he put it." The red haired woman, Charlotte, was laughing now, giddy with how lucky they were to have found their prey.

"Wonderful," Purdue said, taking another step back and nearly tripping over one of the toppled tree trunks. "Just who I was hoping to see. I'm surprised that you and your friends haven't given up by this point. How many times do I have to beat you before you give up and stop bothering me? How many times do I have to make Julian look like a daft buffoon, aye?"

"You have been making fools of us, yes," Lucius said with some resignation. "What you did to Victor and Vincent needs to be answered for. Turning Sasha against us needs to be answered for."

"And you're here to make me pay for those imagined crimes, is that is? Hate to break it to you two, but you're on the wrong side. You work for a complete psychopath. Julian is unstable and you know it."

Lucius gave a shrug. "Perhaps getting rid of you might stabilize him."

There was a snapping branch behind him and Purdue turned around to find other people approaching him, surrounding him. More Black Sun operatives, looking to be the one to put an end to the order's greatest annoyance. Purdue had dealt with members of that group so many times but they had gotten so much more aggressive since Julian's induction as their leader. They weren't afraid to come at him head on. For instance, Lucius and Charlotte could have feigned innocence until the right time to strike but instead, they decided to come at him directly. That was Julian's leadership in action, setting an example for his followers—cutting down whatever was in your way without a moment of hesitation.

But Purdue could also cut down whatever was in the way of his own goals—whether it was a thicket of vines or people trying to end him.

"Julian is going to be so pleased with us," Charlotte said.

Purdue counted all of the enemies that were encircling him: twelve in total, counting Lucius and Charlotte. None of them were armed with any guns and only a handful drew knives or held branches or rocks. With his machete, he could probably take down a couple before being overwhelmed but that wasn't a guarantee and not even an ideal outcome.

The best bet he had would be to get away from them, at least fall back until he could come up with a better plan to take out so many enemies. He looked past a particularly large grunt over to the old Mayan temple that loomed over them nearby. Making for the old structure was his best bet. If he could get inside, he could maybe isolate his enemies or at least fight them in a narrower place where their greater numbers wouldn't matter as much.

"So were you ordered to bring me in dead or alive?" Purdue asked.

"Corvus would prefer alive," Lucius said. "But I'm sure he wouldn't be upset if we brought back your corpse."

"And how upset will he be when you don't bring back anything at all?" Purdue asked with a sly grin before breaking into a full sprint. One of the Black Sun operatives tried to intercept them but he knocked him out of the way and kept running. Purdue didn't bother looking back. He knew they were probably right on his heels. He just stared ahead at the Mayan temple that towered above. That strange building might be the only way he could save himself from this particular predicament.

He reached an opening in the temple and made his way through it, into the dark. It took a few seconds for his eyes to start adjusting to the darkness, especially once he was away from the entryway and completely blanketed by the stone walls around him. The sun had no way to reach inside, making everything nearly impossible to see. That darkness would be helpful in keeping hidden from the Black Sun operatives, though, so he appreciated the lack of lighting inside of the ancient temple.

A beam of light appeared, cutting through the darkness around him. Purdue stayed low, avoiding the ray of light, but then more streams of it illuminated the room. Of course the Order of the Black Sun had come with flashlights. Perfect—there went his small advantage. They couldn't even give him that much.

"Come out here, Purdue!" Lucius shouted. "All of this running and fighting has gotten tiring, hasn't it? You're not going to be able to hide forever. We've always found you in the end, haven't we? Let's just get this over with!"

"I'm good, thanks!" Purdue called back and his voice echoed all throughout the temple, bouncing off the walls. "Why don't you tell me where you're keeping my friends prisoner and then maybe we'll negotiate!"

"Your friends? You mean Dr. Gould? And Jean-Luc Gerard? Or your butler? They're all alive, I can tell you that much...but Corvus is growing impatient. If you don't end this soon, we're just going to have to end them instead. And you deserve to lose that much. You talk about us taking your friends...you have killed a lot of mine! Victor Moore!"

Purdue hadn't killed Victor, not directly or intentionally at least. Victor had wielded a cursed sword that would kill its wielder if he lost possession of the blade. When Purdue had disarmed him, Victor dropped dead and that caused a whole stream of problems for Purdue in getting rid of that sword without dying.

"Vincent! Torsten! Clive!"

Those three tried to assassinate Purdue after Victor's death. They had their own ancient weapons that were imbued with power, and they would have been able to murder Purdue if not for one of the Black Sun's own, Sasha, betraying them and helping Purdue survive.

"Your friends were all terrible, terrible bastards! Murderers and hitmen! My friends did nothing wrong to anyone! That's the difference!"

Purdue's eyes were slowly adjusting to the darkness around him as he crouched down against one of the temple's walls. He did his best not to look at the lights coming from the Black Sun as they walked nearby, all while trying to make sure none of those beams of lights found their way to him. If he could just stay away from them, and stay shrouded by the dark, he might be able to slip past his pursuers. They could be searching for hours in the temple while he made his way out.

He didn't want to abandon exploring the strange place but it might be the only way to survive. He got himself inside of there with the hopes that he could use the temple as an arena, but instead it was only going to be his tomb if he stayed.

Purdue kept low and tried to be light and quiet with each step he took. Lucius continued to try and talk to him, but Purdue stopped answering. The echoes of the chambers might have been helpful in keeping his actual location hidden, but he couldn't risk them hearing which direction he was actually in. His pursuers walked by, their flashlights just narrowly missing him.

He managed to reach the open entrance back toward the sunlight outside, but Charlotte and one other Black Sun operatives were standing guard. Purdue burst forth from the darkness within the temple, catching them off guard. He shoved Charlotte out of his way as he barreled through and slashed at the other operative, cutting the big man in the shoulder with his machete.

"He's here! He's escaping! Get the hell out here!" Charlotte shrieked into the darkness inside the temple before grabbing Purdue by the ankle, bringing him down onto his stomach. His machete went rolling out of his hand on impact, and he tried to pry the woman off of him.

There was a rumble beneath him, a tremor coming up through the ground that went right through his body as he lay there on the rocks. He tried to pry Charlotte's hand off of him, but she had a tight grip. Her hands were like talons. He looked past her toward the temple and saw flashlights within, but the ground beneath them shook even more violently. Charlotte finally noticed the tremors and her eyes widened with concern. Both of their bodies jittered violently and they both realized that they probably weren't safe laying on the ground. Charlotte let go of his leg and the two of them jumped to their feet, taking some steps away from the temple.

The Mayan temple rumbled and groaned. Strange sounds rang out from inside the temple and cracks appeared in the earth, stretching out from the temple to the jungles outside. Purdue half expected the temple to collapse down into the dirt but instead it seemed to be folding in on itself. Despite being made of such old, solid stone, the structure started receding into itself.

The whole surrounding area shook hard like a high-level earthquake was taking place. Purdue and Charlotte could barely stay on their feet and she even used him to keep steady. There were screams from within the temple—Lucius and the other Black Sun grunts.

Reality itself seemed to be tearing apart.

There was a pop—and the temple was gone.

The entire ancient structure disappeared from view. It didn't slip beneath the earth or fly into the sky—it simply wasn't there anymore. Besides the toppled forestry around them, there was no sign that it had even ever been there at all. The temple and presumably Lucius and his cronies inside were gone, and there was no indication of where.

"Lucius!" Charlotte yelled, rushing over to where the temple had just been. She stomped on the dirt, looking around desperately for any sign of her allies, but there was nothing. She looked back to Purdue. "What the hell just happened!?"

"I..." Purdue wanted to give her some sort of witty retort but he couldn't. He was too fixated on his actual surprise over what happened. He didn't pity a murderous woman like Charlotte, but he also couldn't hide his own confusion. "I really have no idea."

"That's not good enough!" Charlotte marched over to him. "You were studying this place! You must know!"

"I didn't have a lot of time to do much research...considering you and your friends decided to try and kill me the second I got here!"

Charlotte let out a frustrated sneer.

"You ruin everything, Purdue!"

"Only for the Order of the Black Sun, it seems."

Purdue turned away and started walking back toward the tree line of the jungle, ready to have to hike back down from where he came from. Charlotte looked baffled when he started to leave and ran after him, grabbing his shoulder. "Where the hell do you think you're going!?"

"There's nothing left for me to study here, is there?"

"You can't leave! We have you! You're coming with us!"

Purdue gave a tired smile and looked past her at the empty space where the Mayan temple had stood minutes earlier. He then looked around in a few other directions. "And who is us, exactly?"

Charlotte's mouth fell open as she suddenly realized just how alone she was. There was no way she was going to be able to drag Purdue back to the Black Sun by herself and they both knew it. She may have had a strong grip when she was holding his ankle, but she didn't seem to be nearly as tough of a fighter as Sasha had been. Purdue smirked, slowly took her hand off of his shoulder and then turned away again.

"Good luck telling Julian Corvus about this," Purdue said. "From everything I've seen, he seems like a very forgiving man. If I was in your shoes, love, I wouldn't go back. I would just find a nice quiet corner of the world and stay there. If I have things my way, the Order of the Black Sun won't be around much longer anyway. Better to jump off that sinking ship now before you get dragged down with it, aye?"

He didn't know Charlotte very well. For all he knew, her loyalty ran very deep and there was no way that he would abandon the order, even if it meant having to deal with Julian's wrath. But, he saw in her expression that she was terrified of failing him and looked a little agreeable to his proposition. He knew in just those few brief moments, that she was a survivor first and foremost and would leave the Order of the Black Sun if it meant that she wouldn't be killed for her failure.

Purdue left her there, among the broken trees, knowing that she wouldn't be going back to Julian. That would be good for him, as she wouldn't be alerting her boss about Purdue's presence there. He didn't need the Black Sun getting any whiff of his location, or he would keep ending up in traps like this one.

He spent the entire walk back through the jungles of Honduras focused on what he had just seen. That Mayan temple had completely dissipated into thin air, leaving nothing. The physics of it didn't make sense. There should have at least been something left behind. An enormous structure like that simply ceased to be—or did it?

A troubling notion was itching at the back of his skull.

If the Mayan temple had suddenly appeared in Honduras one day, without ever having been built there...then it came from somewhere...and clearly that temple could disappear in an instant. It could no doubt reappear then as well. Maybe it would pop back up in that same spot—but it could just as likely reappear in another part of the world. It would just be a matter of where and when.

2

CHAPTER TWO – BIG NEWS FROM THE NORTH

It wasn't every day that someone saw an ancient temple vanish right before their eyes. It was all Purdue could think about. He just kept replaying that moment in his mind over and over again. One moment it had been towering right over him, just as it had been when he cut his way through that jungle. The next second, there was nothing at all. The physics of that just made no sense.

Purdue was sitting in the hotel room he had rented out in New Orleans. He was feeling a little directionless since seeing that temple vanish, and needed an old acquaintance's help to put him back on a clearer path.

For now, he was just doing his best to try and figure out more about the temple he'd seen. It obviously wasn't an ordinary Mayan temple like so many that had been discovered over the years in various states of disrepair. None of those temples had ever just up and disappeared for no reason. He had rented out as many books about Mayans as he could from the libraries in the city and had his laptop almost permanently in front of him to help with his research.

It had taken hours but he finally found a small piece of writing that caught his attention. There was an old Mayan legend about temple that had been built, but no one knew exactly who built it. It would appear one day and then would be gone another. That sounded incredibly familiar. The more he looked into this temple, the most interesting things he learned. For instance, the temple would disappear but reappear in a far-off location soon after. So it didn't just vanish into thin air after all. It traveled somewhere else...like it had teleported away from him, transporting instantaneously to somewhere far away. That confirmed the feeling he had after he watched it vanish. It could indeed reappear.

Some of the Maya called it the 'Moving Temple of Ah Puch'. It frightened many of the tribes back then, but many more went out seeking this temple. Ah Puch was one of the gods of death in their culture and soon after learning the temple's given name, he soon read something even more interesting facts about this mysterious temple.

The Moving Temple of Ah Puch was a temple of sacrifice. Many of the Maya temples were used for such occasion, and those temples' sacrifices were used for various purposes like blessings and for the helpful growth of food and resources. In fact, sacrifice was a big part of the Maya's culture. The most important sacrifices were done with fellow Maya, making human sacrifice somewhat of a normal thing back then for them. They would perform them in all sorts of ways that made Purdue cringe a little as he read about them. Some sacrifices were done with decapitation but those were usually reserved for rival rulers. Another way was with heart extraction, something that the Maya had picked up from the Aztecs. Sometimes the hearts they pulled out were still beating which made Purdue nearly vomit where he sat. Some were sacrificed by being pierced with arrows, or disemboweled, and others were hurled into sinkholes.

All Purdue had determined from his reading was that he was very glad to never have been a human sacrifice. It sounded like an absolutely wretched way to have to go out. If he had to pick between those options though, at least beheading would have been pretty quick.

But while most of the temples' sacrifices were used for mundane reasons, the Moving Temple's sacrifices were used for a far larger purpose. Purdue read the sentence he was on multiple times before he could fully comprehend it. He slowly read it aloud, just in the hopes that speaking it out loud ensured that he wasn't just seeing things.

"The Moving Temple of Ah Puch..." He was probably butchering the pronunciation of that particular god's name but he wasn't the best with linguistics. That was more Dr. Nina Gould's forte, but she wasn't going to be able to help him while she was still trapped as a prisoner... or worse. He wished she was there, but he had to keep moving. It might be the only way to get her back. “The alta

r in the bowels of the Moving Temple of Ah Puch was the site of sacrifices that would be used to grant someone any wish that they desired. That was the true power the gods had given when they forged that temple.”

He read it again, just to be safe and then leaned back where he sat, staring at the pile of books in front of him and the laptop that was, after hours of research, really starting to hurt his eyes. If this was true, then performing a sacrifice at the altar inside that teleporting temple meant that any wish you had would come true. It sounded farfetched but at the same time, the idea of an old temple that could pop in and out of existence was just as strange. If that part of it was true, then so could the part about the sacrifices and the wishes they could grant inside.

If he could get back to that temple—wherever the hell it was—then he might have a chance to make a wish inside. And if that wish really did come true, it could solve all of the many problems that had been plaguing his life in recent days.

This was his chance to fix everything. He could stop the Order of the Black Sun without having to get into a war. He could maybe even get his friends out of there. Hell, if it really granted any wish, he could maybe even completely fix the entire world. It could absolutely be bullshit but it had far too much potential to just pass up. He had to at least try.

Purdue kept up his research for the next few hours, but it felt like days. He learned all he could about the Moving Temple of Ah Puch but there wasn't much more to go off of. It was a legend that had been passed down orally through time. There was the occasional sighting over the centuries that stood out. One story came from a Spanish explorer during the sixteenth century, back when contact between the Spaniards and the Maya had first taken place. One man saw the temple from their ship and when he told his fellow sailors to look at it, he watched it vanish. It was incredible that the Moving Temple of Ah Puch had managed to stay under the radar for so long, especially nowadays with the creation of satellite images mapping out most of the planet.

He had hoped to find something that would indicate just how often this Mayan temple stayed in one place but there wasn't nearly enough research done. In fact, there was hardly any research at all. He spent most of his time just re-reading the same few tidbits he had managed to find. For the most part, the Moving Temple of Ah Puch remained nothing more than an ancient legend that no one really took too much notice of.

For most of his time researching, he had the TV

in the room on for no other reason than to have some background noise. He hadn't heard a single thing that had been spoken. It was just chatter that was being drowned out by all of the research passing through his skull. He was absolutely waterlogged with everything he was learning but hearing one word seemed to breathe new life into him.

"A temple."

The reporter on the news said the word and for the first time in hours, Purdue looked up from all of his studies. He fumbled for the TV remote which was buried under his piles of rented books, and turned up the volume as loud as he could. It took a moment for his eyes to adjust from reading so much writing to seeing images on the TV but when he did, he saw a very familiar sight on the screen. Except this time, he wasn't looking at a jungle. He was staring at the sprawling white vastness of the Arctic.

The reporter's commentary continued and Purdue was glad to actually be listening this time. "A Russian researcher studying global warming from a camp up in the region discovered the sight early this morning at daybreak."

Purdue watched the news helicopters circle the ancient structure; it was a marvel that shouldn't have been able to ever be in that spot but Purdue had seen it before, very recently in Honduras. And that temple looked just like the one he had seen before—identical even. There was no doubt about it. He was staring directly at the Moving Temple of Ah Puch.

The newscasters spoke again. "From what we are hearing, this structure has never been seen up here until today. Despite satellite footage and well documented imaging of this landscape, it has somehow avoided detection, almost as if it is new to the area. Another marine biologist studying the waters in this region claims that the structure popped up here this morning, seemingly from nowhere. While some are claiming that climate change unearthed it from the ice, others refute that theory with visual evidence that disputes that notion. If we examine the chart showing melting--"

Purdue stopped listening to her voice, but couldn't look away from the video footage of the temple. It was the same—exactly the same as it had looked when it vanished into thin air in the jungle. It had somehow traversed from South America to the Arctic, probably in mere seconds—or even instantaneously. Something like that shouldn't have been scientifically possible...but it happened. He'd seen it happen. That Mayan temple had teleported from one hemisphere to another.

It was just like the legends had said...but so soon...he wasn't expecting to ever even see that temple again but if he did, it wouldn't be for quite some time. And now the whole world was going to see how strange this particular Mayan creation was.

Purdue picked up the phone and immediately called Sam Cleave.

He would need backup this time.

The phone rang a few times in his ear before he heard the familiar voice of his friend.

"What do you want, Purdue?"

"You don't sound very happy to hear from me," Purdue laughed. He knew that Sam could sometimes be a bit grouchy, especially when he wasn't sure if his time was being wasted yet. "I can assure you that you're going to like what you hear."

There was some noise on the other end of the phone and Purdue could have sworn that he heard a woman's voice somewhere in the background. Perhaps Sam was with someone and Purdue was interrupting a rather intimate moment. That was awkward, but at the same time, Sam needed to start thinking with his upstairs brain again and remember what they were really trying to accomplish. They had captured friends waiting for them. There wasn't time to waste with matters like relations with the opposite sex. Purdue loved a nice date as much as the next man, but it would be impossible for him to enjoy knowing that a secret society was out to kill him, had stolen all of his belongings, and were probably torturing people who were important to him.

"You with someone?" He asked bluntly.

"What does it matter? Shut up."

"So that's a yes."

"What do you want?" He was definitely more irritable than usual—and that probably meant he was with a woman. Sam had never had the best luck in that department, putting it mildly. It was one of the unfortunate truths about being such an investigative mind—trust issues.

"I just wanted to tell you what I've been up to lately," Purdue said. "A little catch up, aye?"

"Can't we do it another time?"

"No, no, there's no time to waste," Purdue said. "You might have been wondering where I've been."

"Haven't really noticed you were gone."

"Charming, but let me continue. I've been researching a Mayan temple that appeared one day in Honduras. It hadn't been there up until very recently...so I went there myself to see it with my own two eyes. The Black Sun was there by the way, but I'm fine, thanks for asking. Anyway, the temple up and vanished right before my eyes. Poof. Gone."

"The hell you talking about? It disappeared?"

"Aye, didn't you just hear me? Poof. Just like that."

"So all of the research you've been doing on it was for nothing."

"No, no, Sam. Must you always be so cynical?"

"Yes," he cut in real quick.

"I've learned quite a lot. I've learned that temple has been popping up all over the world for hundreds of years in all kinds of places. Never for long, but long enough for some to see it. But by the time they try to really get a good look at it, it's nowhere to be found. It teleports. I don't know how and I don't know why but it's constantly on the move."

"Okay..." Sam still didn't seem overly enthused by the story.

"That's not even the most exciting part, if you believe it. No, the legends go far beyond just it moving around all over the world. There's something about this place obviously, but something even more. There are stories that if you perform a sacrifice at the altar founding this particular moving temple...well...you get whatever you want."

"Meaning?"

"Exactly as it sounds," Purdue said, and was satisfied hearing a little bit of interest coming from Sam. "You perform the sacrifice at the altar, and the temple's power—or the gods or whatever the hell it is—will grant you one wish in exchange for the sacrifice. If the legends are true, then there's no limits to the wish. You want the meaning of it...well the meaning is that we could fix everything that's gone wrong. We could free our friends, get rid of the Order of the Black Sun, or even just get ourselves our dream lives. All in an instant. We won't have to cut our way through legions of bastards to hopefully come out with a win in the end."

Sam wasn't quite as resistant now. That aspect of the Moving Temple of Ah Puch was enough to ease his skepticism, but he still wasn't entirely convinced.

"And you think it's true?"

Purdue did, but he didn't want to sound too

enthusiastic or he might spook Sam from hearing him out.

"Who knows until we try?"

"And why has no one else done anything with this?"

"It isn't exactly easy to track down the place. It could be anywhere at any time. But listen, Sam, this is too good of an opportunity that we can't let go to waste. If the stories about the altar inside that temple are true...then..."

"I know," Sam said irritably. "You don't need to explain again. I know what that might mean for us. It could change everything. This run of bad luck could finally turn around. I get it."

"Good," Purdue said. "So you're coming."

He didn't make it sound like a request, because it really wasn't. He needed Sam's help on this one and their list of alternative allies to assist him had grown remarkably short in recent days.

Sam was silent on the line for a moment and Purdue could just picture him shaking his head. Whoever Sam was with must have been quite the woman but Purdue knew that Sam's loyalty to Nina and the others was too strong to completely spit in the face of. He had to come along; all it took was just a wee bit of convincing.

"Fine."

"Brilliant," Purdue said, filling with excitement. He stared at the television screen where the temple was sitting in the Arctic. Part of him felt like the Moving Temple of Ah Puch was going to wait for them, it needed to. If that temple wanted to make a really good wish, then they were the perfect ones to come for a visit. "I'll send you the details of where we should meet soon. I just have to make a quick stop first."

"A quick stop where?"

"I'll explain later," Purdue said with a laugh. "I just want to make sure that we at least have some idea what we're in for up there in the Arctic."

Purdue was glad to have Sam by his side once again. He was one of his oldest colleagues and despite butting heads some times and having some opposing viewpoints here and there, he knew that Sam was reliable and trustworthy. Plus, the two of them made a pretty good team when they found themselves backed into a corner.

JULIAN CORVUS WAS STILL TRYING to get used to receiving reports from those beneath him in the Order of the Black Sun. It was one of the parts of leadership that he had been dreading the most and it was just about as tedious as he expected it to be when he took over the secret society. There were so many things that just didn't interest him, or seemed superfluous. How many cursed shrunken heads did they need? How many sacred talismans? How many holy weapons? The only ones that mattered in the end were the ones that could be useful to their future goals, and those were few and far between.

Right now, the Black Sun had more pressing concerns, and he appreciated that the current report at least had more connections to his actual interests than most of the ones he heard. It helped that he didn't hate who was presenting the report.

Boris was nothing more than a low-ranking grunt within the Order of the Black Sun, but Julian saw something in him—a spark of something more useful. Boris had a way with computers and surveillance so naturally that Julian put him in charge of monitoring the order's activities all around the world. He sometimes was a little too proud of his work, but he was good at it so Julian couldn't fault him too much.

"We haven't heard a status report from Lucius or Charlotte," Boris said. "They were stationed out of Honduras, part of the web you set up for Purdue."

Julian was well aware that they were part of his network that he had put in place. He had his operatives spread all over the world at any historical hot spots that might catch David Purdue's attention; old unexplored caverns, lost citadels, and abandoned burial grounds. In this case, a strange temple that had appeared out of nowhere. They were small teams scattered, but he hoped they would be enough to at least alert him of Purdue's whereabouts or even bring him in as a prisoner.

But alas, he'd grown to know his enemy more than that.

"So I imagine that he fell right into that web then...and being Purdue...probably immediately set fire to it. Burnt the entire thing down. Every thread we put up is gone."

Julian wasn't surprised by Purdue's tenacity anymore, and he was even less surprised by his underlings' utter incompetence. He had come to terms with the fact that if Purdue was outnumbered ten to one by even the most high-ranking members of the Black Sun, he would most likely find a way to come out on top in the end. It was what made him such a dangerous opponent—Purdue always found a way, no matter the odds.

Julian had underestimated him once; took his things and left him to burn in his own house. It had felt like a real victory at the time but sure enough, Purdue bounced back and had cheated death yet again. Julian knew better than that now, and if he ever thought Purdue was dead again, he would be sure to check and be certain that it was true this time.

Now, it was just a matter of getting him.

"We sent a drone out to their location to check on Lucius and Charlotte."

"And it never came back, did it?" Julian guessed, knowing it was completely possible that Purdue had brought one of those little robots down.

However, he was immediately proven wrong. "It did...but there was nothing there. No sign of Lucius.

No sign of Charlotte. No sign of Purdue. Not even any sign of that temple that they were stationed at."

Julian's curiosity was more than piqued by that last part. "What do you mean?"

"The temple that had supposedly only been there only a short period of time...it's gone."

"Elaborate," Julian said, not fully wrapping his head around that notion. "What do you mean it's gone? Someone tore it down and moved on?"

"Unlikely. It seems more like it just vanished into thin air."

"Ancient buildings don't just vanish into thin air."

"True," Boris said, looking pleased that they were on the same page. "But they also aren't supposed to be able to just appear out of the blue either...but this one did according to everyone who lived in that jungle. If it can appear out of nowhere —then who's to say that it can't just disappear right back into nowhere too?"

Julian was intrigued but mostly still focused on Purdue. There was a possibility that they were connected. Perhaps Purdue was inside of that temple when it miraculously disappeared. He did go to Honduras after all; he took the bait just like Julian knew he would and went to investigate something unusual. Maybe that Mayan temple had disintegrated into nothing and taken Purdue with it. That would solve most of Julian's problems. He would just have to wait and see. If Purdue was out there, he'd be coming soon enough, considering that the Order of the Black Sun still had his little friends as prisoners. Purdue was already making preparations to try and rescue them. From everything Julian had heard, Purdue had been gallivanting all over the globe, trying to recover his funds and finding new items to use against the Black Sun. If Purdue hadn't dissipated with that temple, and that inevitable fight was still coming, then Julian couldn't wait.

After all of the trouble Purdue had caused them, and especially after Julian's own blunder of beating him but not killing him, they needed to get rid of him for good.

Another agent burst into Julian's office. He nearly murdered the grunt right there on the spot for daring to barge in like that and interrupt but something on the young man's face told him that it was an emergency.

"I'm so sorry, sir, but you may want to turn on the news. Everyone is talking about it."

"Talking about what?" Julian asked, still fighting the urge to murder the man. "Spit it out."

"It's a temple in the Arctic, sir."

3

CHAPTER THREE – THE PERFECT GIRLFRIEND

Sam hung up the phone. He'd gotten calls from David Purdue so many times, but this one felt different than all of the others that had come before. There was a tension between the phone lines, like both men knew how dangerous their world was right now. But Purdue was right: that temple's power might be able to fix everything. They might not even have to actually fight the Order of the Black Sun anymore. It all depended on if the stories about that place were true.

"What's wrong?"

Kendra looked at him with some concern. They hadn't been together long—they weren't even an official item or anything—but he was always smitten by how beautiful she looked.

"Nothing," Sam fibbed, pulling her into his arms. "Everything is perfect."

"No, really," she giggled. "You can tell me, you know?"

Sam relented. He would feel guilty if he kept lying to her. "I just have to leave for a little while. I'm not sure when I'll be back..."

"Going off on another adventure with that rich friend of yours? David, right?"

"Yeah...I hope it's not too much of an adventure, though. A nice leisurely expedition would be nice for a change."

Kendra put a hand on his cheek, looking worried. "Are you going someplace dangerous?"

Sam wanted to tell her no, to reassure her that everything was going to be fine, but he knew better than to ever assume how one of these journeys with Purdue would end up. There was no way to really tell what would be ahead or how bad it could be. So many of their trips ended with risking their lives, running from danger, or having to fight the Order of the Black Sun.

Still, he didn't want to worry Kendra.

"I don't think so," Sam said. "No, I think this time is just going to be some reconnaissance work. Only looking around at that temple that popped up in the Arctic."

"I saw something about that! That's so weird."

"It is," Sam said. "It gets even weirder. Purdue says that this temple will grant you your heart's desire if you perform a sacrifice inside. Sounds crazy to me, but that rich bastard has proven me wrong before...I guess he's not all that rich these days...but still. So we're probably just going to take a look around and see what's going on."

Kendra looked somewhat sad about his news but it only flashed for a moment before turning into a smile. Even when she was upset, she still was willing to put that aside to make things easier for him. That was a wonderful trait that she had. She wasn't selfish or clingy or anything like that. He would have to make it up to her when he returned.

"Be very careful...and pack warm."

"Of course," Sam said. "You going to be waiting for me when I get back?"

"Maybe," Kendra said with a wink. "Though, I can't make any promises, especially if some other well-traveled man comes storming into my life while you're gone."

Sam really hoped that didn't happen. His time with Kendra had been some of the best times he'd had in a long time. Especially given how much of an insane turn the rest of his life took. He needed those moments with her, to just enjoy life and not let all of the garbage with the Order of the Black Sun and ancient artifacts get him down. He didn't want to rush things, but he was constantly surprised by just how wonderful of a companion she was.

Sam started packing his belongings, and Kendra was quick to lend him a hand. They may have taken a break or two just to say a proper goodbye to one another, but soon enough he was nearly ready to go. He'd gone on so many expeditions with Purdue, but usually he didn't have much to look forward to coming home to. Now there was someone who inspired him to get the job with Purdue done.

Kendra was perfect and he loved everything about her, but he couldn't voice it out loud. He was scared he would sound like he was moving too fast and scare her off. He had to keep his admiration in check, and not go over the top. Maybe after all of this and a little time apart, those feelings would just grow even stronger. That was how the saying went after all: parting makes the heart grow fonder.

"So you'll be here when I get back?"

Kendra just giggled. "Of course I will be. Just don't freeze your ass off up there! It's a nice ass, and I feel like frostbite wouldn't do it any favors."

Sam grinned. "I'll do my best to protect this asset."

"Appreciated."

They shared another parting kiss before Sam turned to leave his place. She already had a key to it so he didn't have to worry about leaving her there. Maybe things were moving too fast, but who was he to question it? Who was anyone to question it? There was no magic formula that dictated what was really the right time to do anything, especially when it came to relationships of the heart. He was happier than he had been in a long time.

Even if this Moving Temple of Ah Puch contained the altar that could grant any wish, Sam didn't have to worry about wishing for anything for himself. There was no need for some ancient Maya legend to give him what he wanted. He already had it. No Mayan temple could give him another Kendra.

As much as he enjoyed his trips with Purdue, and as much as he was hopeful that this could be what finally saved Nina and also got rid of Julian Corvus and the Order of the Black Sun, he couldn't help but feel more excited by the idea of seeing Kendra again. He didn't know how long this one would be. It was impossible to ever know how long these adventures might last or if he would even get through it alive at all. But if he did make it back, no matter how long it had been, he really hoped Kendra would be there. He couldn't wait to see her again.

THE DOOR to Sam Cleave's current home closed behind him, and she listened to his car pull out of the driveway as he went off on another one of the adventures he liked to tell her about so much. But those adventures weren't very impressive compared to some of the things she had been through. He'd never been assigned the missions that she had been assigned by the Order of the Black Sun.

Kendra had to admit, there was a certain joy seeing how Sam Cleave's eyes lit up every time he looked at her. He was so entranced by everything about her, and why wouldn't he be? She worked hard on the performance she gave, harder than most of the world's best actors probably did. There was more at stake in her roles; no camera to appeal to, no audience to impress, and no script to memorize. She had to truly become that character, to make any other person in the scene believe that it was real, to not even know that all they were doing was playing in a scene that only she knew the last line of.

Sam Cleave may not have said it, but he was head over heels for her. He had been the instant she started speaking to him. He may have seen a lot of things in his career, and been through all kinds of hardships, but that just made him even easier to manipulate. He tried to act jaded and experienced, but really he only wanted someone to love him, to make him feel needed. No amount of trips with the infamous David Purdue could replace how good she could make him feel. There was a difference between time spent with a friend and time spent with someone that you were in love with. It was a somewhat slight distinction, but it could make all the difference.

She may have even felt a little bad about using him if he wasn't so stupid. He made it far too easy for her. When Julian Corvus had assigned her the task, she thought it was going to be difficult but it was one of the easiest things that she had ever done. She just had to bat her eyelashes, give him a few kisses, hold his hand here and there, and offer him comforting words to make him feel good about himself and even better about her. It was a simple script to know. She could almost predict all of the pathetically sappy things he was going to say before he even started speaking them.

Once she had played along with those small prompts and done all of those things, that buffoon would tell her anything; not because she asked him to but because he felt like he could. He had someone who he could talk to without any judgment being passed. Little did he know that she was judging him all the time.

Kendra was his safe space where he could be honest and sincere with all of those little feelings he had. He had no idea how unsafe of a space it really was.

The secrets he shared weren't secrets at all anymore once they reached her ears—they were information at that point, and those former secrets then belonged to the Order of the Black Sun from that moment forward.

And the information he had just given her was no different.

Kendra pulled out her phone and dialed the number for the leader of the order. Julian would probably be happy with what she had to say. He usually was. Compared to the rest of her colleagues and co-workers, she had a great track record for actually being useful to the Black Sun. She knew what was needed and didn't waste anyone's time like so many of the others did. When Kendra called, Julian knew that he was going to be listening to something of actual value to his plans.

"Yes."

It was Julian's usual greeting when he answered the phone. It wasn't a 'hello' and it certainly wasn't a 'how are you'; it was more like he was telling whoever was calling that he was listening, and that he better like what he heard. It was expectant and probably made most of his other underlings uneasy, but not Kendra. To her, Julian was the man that had given her the world, given her a purpose, and put her gifts to actual good use. She was far too grateful to him to be afraid of him. She owed him far too much.

"It's Kendra." There was no response but she never expected one. She knew that this was presentation time and not an actual conversation. "I have some new information about David Purdue. He and Sam Cleave are traveling to some Mayan temple that's in the Arctic right now...if that makes any sense. It's strange but that's what he said. Turn on the TV and I'm sure you will see all about it. Purdue told him that it was in Honduras recently but that he's certain this one in the Arctic is the same one." She was rambling, which she sometimes did when she wasn't sure what exactly she was talking about. It was tough to know what to say when you didn't fully understand what you were trying to describe. She tried to get it back on track. "I don't know how that temple is moving, but that wasn't the most interesting part to me. Purdue seems to think that there's an altar inside, and if you perform a sacrifice on it, the temple will grant a wish. Any wish."

Again, there was no response at first but Julian hadn't hung up yet, which meant he was interested at least. If he didn't somewhat enjoy what she was saying, then he would have hung up by that point.

"They're going to be on their way there very soon if you want to beat them to it."

"I appreciate your hard work, Kendra." He always said that and it never sounded entirely genuine. "If you're right, then this may be the time we can finally settle this. And once it's settled and done with, you can move on to something fresh to sink those remarkably sharpened teeth into. Something more worthy of your gifts."

She appreciated the compliment, but coming from Julian, it still felt somewhat hollow. He was just telling her what she wanted to hear, giving her a pat on the back for giving him something he could at least think about a little bit.

Even his offer didn't feel as great as she would have thought.

"Aw that's a shame. I've enjoyed my time playing with Sammy."

"Mr. Cleave is a tool to get to Purdue. The moment Purdue is gone is the moment Mr. Cleave no longer has any reason to live."

Kendra expected as much but she really would miss some of her time with Sam. He was more fun than most of the people she had acted with before. It was a shame that he would have to go. He wasn't all bad in the sack either, especially when compared to some of the other people in the past that she had to grow close with for work. Maybe Julian would let her say goodbye to Sam before he was put down. She wasn't sure if she would keep up the act for Sam until the very end, playing the crying and devastated lover role. Perhaps she could finally come out of character and tell him the truth just as he died. That sounded like a good time to her. The look on his face alone might be priceless.

"Be easy to contact," Julian ordered. "We may have further use of your talents where we are going."

That got Kendra excited again. She wasn't going to be sitting at home waiting for her fake boyfriend to come crawling back after all. If Julian needed her in the next phase of his plans, it would have to be to do something new, something thrilling. Maybe it wouldn't be a new role altogether, but perhaps a brand new interesting scene to learn.

4

CHAPTER FOUR – THE HIDDEN KEY

Nina sat in the dark and dank little cell that she had grown so accustomed to. She'd lost count of how many days she had been the Order of the Black Sun's prisoner. It was hard to tell when tomorrow came when she couldn't even see a glimpse of the outside world. There was no day or night for her anymore. Everything just melded together into a crippling, depressing blur.

But there was finally some hope. She looked at the key that Elijah Dane had given her—the key to her escape. She examined it often, and slept with it held tightly in her hand. She had tried escaping before and that hadn't ended well at all. It was a complete disaster. She had to be more careful this time, since it could be the only real chance of escape she ever got. She couldn't let the key go to waste.

Purdue was still out there, alive and continuing

his fight with the Black Sun. Maybe she could use that as the perfect distraction. She and Purdue might still be able to work together, even so far away and without even fully realizing it.

She heard the corridor door swing open. As footsteps approached, she placed the key on the floor and put one foot on top of it. It would be a lot harder for her visitor to spot with her standing on top of it.

Julian appeared on the other side of the cell bars, and Nina instantly grew more nervous. Julian had that effect; he was sadistic and unpredictable, terribly scary traits for a captor to have.

Julian didn't say anything at first, but he looked on edge. That calm and confident persona he liked to put on was nowhere to be found.

"You don't look so good..." Nina said, being sure that she kept all of her body weight down on the key under her sole. "Terrible actually, and you weren't very good looking to begin with, if we're all being honest."

"I have had better days, yes." Julian seemed distant, and still hadn't even looked at her. He kept his wide gaze to the floor. Thankfully, the part of the floor he was looking at wasn't near her foot. He leaned his head against the cell bars. "Your friend Mr. Purdue is such...such an irritating little man. I have been all over the world, met thousands of people from all kinds of cultures...but he remains the most aggravating person I've ever had the pleasure of meeting."

"He's always been stubborn," Nina said with a shrug. She didn't have a shred of sympathy for Julian. Usually, Purdue's more obnoxious tendencies might have irritated her, but she was relishing that they were obviously giving Julian a whole lot of frustration.

"Indeed..." Julian ran his fingers along the bars. "To be honest, Dr. Gould, I've started to contemplate if killing you would be the best option."

Nina's heart immediately started racing, pumping away inside her, screaming at her to start panicking but she held it in as best as she could. She might not even have the chance to use the key. She did everything to keep her composure but it was dwindling away with every second. She was helpless if he decided that killing her was his best choice.

"I think that sounds like a really bad decision," Nina said, keeping calm enough to sound brave.

"You would think that, wouldn't you?" Julian let out a humorless laugh before biting it back into a sharp sneer. "We're about to end this feud with David Purdue once and for all. And sometimes the best way to defeat an enemy is by inflicting as much pain as possible...to start creating casualties...important casualties even. And you would seem to be the perfect candidate for such a casualty, no?"

Nina swallowed her fear. "No. I think that that I would be terrible at it."

Julian's gray gaze was finally upon her and she wished he would avert it back to the floor again. Those icy eyes could break anyone's composure. He didn't see a person when he was looking at you—he only saw a future corpse that might be able to benefit his ambitions.

She might only have seconds left before he decided to end her. She didn't want to die in a cramped little holding cell down in the dark where no one would ever find her. She didn't want to be killed by a man that she stabbed through the heart once, who shouldn't even be alive right now. She wanted to live for years to come, free of all of the horrors she'd had to endure since being taken by the Black Sun.

But she might not get that chance now. All she could do was hope that Julian Corvus remained unpredictable, and would decide to yet again change his mind and spare her. She hated being at his mercy, but it was all she could be right now.

Julian grinned, his face pressed against the bars. There was such a thin membrane between Julian and Nina, and she could feel his evil starting to spill the cell. "I don't know...I think it might be worth a try."

That was it. He was going to kill her then.

His decision was made.

The door down the hall opened, drawing Julian's attention away from her. She felt a surge of relief when his cold eyes withdrew from her. A few moments later, Elijah Dane appeared. He only flashed a fleeting glance in Nina's direction before adjusting the glasses on his nose like he always did.

"We've received an update from Kendra."

Julian glared at Elijah. "Can't you see I'm in the middle of a very important conversation?"

"Apologies for the interruption," Elijah said with his usual passiveness. "She said it was urgent. Sam Cleave finally gave her some information that we could actually use."

Nina's attention perked up at the sound of Sam's name. Until now, she hadn't been sure if Sam was even alive, but, for all she knew, he was on the other side of this facility in some other holding cell. Maybe he was being interrogated. But the way Elijah was talking made it seem like Sam was outside somewhere.

"And what did she learn?"

Elijah flashed another quick glance at Nina but she couldn't quite read his expression. "David Purdue's next destination."

"Excellent," Julian said. A sick smile stretched across Julian's face. He turned to Nina, still wearing that disturbed glee on his face. "Perhaps it's not quite time to kill you just yet, Dr. Gould."

Julian stormed out, beckoning for Elijah to follow him. Before he did, Elijah looked at Nina with a silent warning to proceed carefully but to not let the key that he gave her go to waste.

5

CHAPTER FIVE – THE RETURN OF MAMA MAY AND UNCERTAIN FUTURES

Purdue hadn't been to New Orleans since his search for the Book of Shadows. Back when he had very, very little experience with morbid spell books and magical hexes. It was a new challenge for him at the time. That particular misadventure had happened just before the decisive attack by the Order of the Black Sun that destroyed his finances, his home, and his dignity. At that point, Jean-Luc Gerard wasn't a prisoner, and was a simple owner of a very well-respected occult book shop. Jean had been Purdue's guide through the French Quarter of the city and had introduced him to the supernatural underbelly of New Orleans. Part of his tour was bringing Purdue to an old psychic who was revered for her legitimate gifts of foresight—Mama May.

When Purdue first met Mama May, naturally he didn't believe that all of her fortune telling and hocus pocus was real. The more he looked back on the predictions that she told him though, the more he realized how accurate all of her visions and proclamations had been. She had seen the dark turn his life was going to take soon after their meeting. She warned him about a "dead man" who he had since realized was Julian Corvus—and that the dead man was following him. At that point, he had thought he was rid of Julian forever, but sure enough that dead man really was out to get him. Even with that warning, he hadn't seen Julian's attack coming.

And the most significant words Mama May had said over and over still rang in his head. She had said the words "riches to rags" nearly one hundred times. And that had proven to be her most accurate prediction. He had billions of dollars the last time he visited Mama May. He had his entire collection of artifacts. He had a private jet and could buy just about anything in the world. And in moments, after the Black Sun's attack, he had lost it all. Riches to rags, indeed.

Purdue would usually have rolled his eyes at the idea of a psychic foreseeing his future, but Mama May proved to him that she was the real deal. Jean once told him that he used to visit her any time he was going to be traveling, to at least have a small idea about what might be laying ahead of him. Purdue had retained that piece of advice and now planned to do the same.

Given that the war with Julian Corvus and the Order of the Black Sun was likely imminent, it seemed like a good time to go back to Mama May's and heed whatever future she had for him this time. Unfortunately, with Jean captive, he didn't have the respect and connections that Jean had in the city. Purdue had to wait in line with all of the other people who wanted Mama May to show them what their futures held in store. He waited hours before it was finally his time to meet his destiny.

Purdue stepped into the house and when she saw him walk in, the frail woman looked at him with some recognition, but there wasn't any excitement or even surprise. There was just a moment of understanding and then she looked away, like he wasn't even there at all.

"I did not expect to see your face again. You look very different than the last time we spoke. Even the way you entered...you move in a new fashion. I would not call it gracefulness, no, but it was something different and unexpected..."

"Aye," Purdue said. "I feel much different than the last time I was here. You could say that I have been through a hell of a lot since then. I paddled my way through a proper shit storm, I can tell you that much."

"So the vultures came for your belongings, after all."

"You knew that they would."

The woman snickered. "I saw what might happen, not a guarantee that it would. Remember, I can only see what may happen. I can't determine which path fate will take in the end. But yours...yes yours was interesting. I remember all of your possibilities seemed bleak, no matter what happened. More vivid than most people. More painful..."

Purdue recalled the way she had thrashed about during her vision of his future. Jean had said that it wasn't usually that intense, but something about what she saw in Purdue's future had put her into a frenzy. And now he could see why. Hindsight truly did have perfect perspective.

"It was painful, aye," Purdue said. "You look surprised that I'm still even alive."

"I am," she said bluntly "I sensed death all around you. It was everywhere. Many people come here, wanting to know if they will overcome their demons but your demons are different than the rest, aren't they? Your demons live and breathe on their own. They don't live in your head. No. They walk the Earth. They are actively working to see you dead, and they have horrible plans for the rest of us."

It was still alarming how much Mama May knew. He didn't know how she had these abilities nor where they came from but they were just as impressive as they had been the first time. She was no swindler or con artist. She was the only true seer he had ever met in all of his many travels.

"And why is it that you have come back for another visit? Surely you didn't come all of this way to exchange small talk with me. There are many who require my services. Their time is just as valuable to me as yours. Perhaps, if Jean-Luc had accompanied you..." She looked past him, just to prove her point. "But he has not."

"He can't," Purdue said firmly. "That's part of why I'm here. Jean was with me when my whole life came crashing down around me. He got caught in the crossfire and was taken prisoner."

Mama May looked disappointed to hear that. Jean was very popular in the community and a friend to Mama May.

"I have to say...it had been some time since I heard anything from him..."

An idea came to Purdue and he figured he should at least ask. "There's not any way for you to detect if he's still alive at least, is there? Use some sort of magic to find him...?"

"I'm a seer, young man, not a wizard. And my sight only extends so far. You came to me because you wanted to know what you might be facing in the near future, yes? I can tell you that much, but I can't promise it will be anything good and I can't--"

"Guarantee it will even happen the way you see it," Purdue finished for her. "Aye, I know. But I'd rather have an idea of one possible outcome than no idea about any of them."

Mama May nodded and pulled out a slim knife from under her table. It had seemed so threatening the first time he came to visit, and even now it was unnerving to see that frail little woman drawing a knife on him. But at least this time, he knew what the knife's real purpose was.

"You have done this before. You know how it works."

That was true. Purdue held his hand out, opening his palm, ready for the first part of her ritual. When the knife came, slicing open his skin and spilling blood from his hand, he wasn't startled like the first time. This was how her visions worked. She pushed Purdue's hand into a fist, letting blood droplets seep out onto the table. It was just like before; Mama May kept holding his hand while she stared at the blood that started to pool in front of her.

That was where her visions came from—the blood. She could almost read it, and it showed her so many things that could happen to its owner. He didn't know if the amount of the blood made a difference, or if maybe the blood type showed different things. But his blood apparently didn't contain any good possibilities.

She was trembling, and it was growing worse the more she looked at his blood on the table.

"The place you are going is cold."

She wasn't wrong about that. The Arctic wasn't exactly a sauna this time of year, or any time of year. If that was all she had to offer this time, then he was wasting his time. He could have predicted that the Arctic would be cold too. He already had.

"Yes, very cold. Cold as death itself. You and so many others will be colder than you have ever been. Cold forever. Frozen forever. Stuck. Yes, stuck."

She squeezed his hand tighter, pressing right down on the open wound in his palm. He winced from the pain but she didn't seem to care. She just kept tightening her grip, but she wasn't focused on him. She was still fixated on the blood that was dropping down to the table.

"The place you are going will be infested with evil. It is the same evil that you have come across before. The dead man still walks. He will keep walking for eternity if left to his own devices. And he will walk in a world that is his own, and he will walk by many bowing before him."

None of that sounded good at all. So, Julian would be walking a world that he ruled; he could conquer the world at some point. Purdue couldn't imagine that it would be a good world.

Purdue pushed through the searing pain in his hand. He needed to try to learn more about his allies that were taken. They were what would make this battle worth it. She might not have been able to tell him if they were alive, but maybe she could see if they were even part of his future at all. "What about Nina? Jean? Charles? What about them? Do you see them!?"

Mama May was quivering, still squeezing his hand hard.

"There is a key. A key. Yes, a key and it is unlocking a cage. Inside the cage there is...a cage...a glass cage. A cage full of darkness. You can see it through the glass and it can see you. It can see you!

It is entrapped! Trying to shatter its container! Do not let it! Do not let it!"

"I won't!" Purdue said through his clenched teeth as she kept squeezing his hand. He felt like he was going to run out of blood at some point and pass out if she kept this up. It was like she was draining all of the blood from his body. The future was sapping his life force away and it was going to take all of his blood in exchange for her visions.

"There is more. More. More. More. There is a man...a man standing on...standing on the sun. A darkened sun that does not shine very bright. This man is standing on this sun looking down on it. He wants to change its shine. He wants to change its intensity. He wants to change the sun. But no one can change the sun. They can't touch it. They can barely look at it. It can't be changed! It can't be changed!"

It just sounded like gibberish now. He knew there must have been more to it but all of it was so vague. A man standing on the sun wasn't exactly scientifically possible so he wasn't sure how much stock he should put in that vision. It probably wasn't going to happen, at least any time in the next few hundred years. Whatever man was standing on the sun was no doubt melting and burning to a crisp. Then again, she had mentioned it was a darkened sun—a black sun. Someone was standing on top of the black sun...it had to be Julian. He probably would have liked that image. It almost seemed godlike, and he knew Julian Corvus well enough to know that he would have loved having that distinction.

"Please, what about my friends?"

"Your friends..." Mama May somehow looked even more distant than she had before. She leaned in close to the blood, practically touching it with her nose, like she was trying to find the answers deep in its red hue. Like Nina, Jean, and Charles were somewhere in that blood, drowning inside.

"There will be many faces in the cold. So many faces. They all have their own reasons for being there, and those reasons will put blades into their hands. There will be many blades, as many as there are faces. And those many blades are piercing many backs. Yes. Many blades piercing many backs." Her voice was growing louder, and her posture more frantic. She was seeing something bad, something very, very bad.

"Many blades piercing many backs! Many blades piercing many backs! Many blades piercing many backs! They are being sharpened! Sharpened! Sharp enough to cut through souls! Sharp enough to change the world! Many blades piercing many backs!"

Purdue tried to pull away but she wouldn't let him. Her grip was so strong for such a frail little woman, but maybe the power coursing through her wasn't just showing her the future. Maybe it was filling her petite body with a drive to make sure that her message was hard. She couldn't allow him to pull away. He needed to hear the rest of what she had to say.

"There will be a sacrifice!"

Purdue stopped trying to resist her warnings now. He hadn't mentioned anything to her about the Mayan temple or its power, yet she seemed to know about the legends of the sacrificial altar. He needed to know about it.

"A sacrifice!"

"Yes," Purdue admitted but he doubted she could even hear him past her own yelling. "Yes I know about the sacrifice already. But what will the sacrifice be!? What is going to be used to make the wish? What are we going to have to lose?"

"Something you would not expect. A true sacrifice. Sacrifices are not easy! Sacrifices are not easy! Sacrifices are not easy!"

She kept yelling the same phrase over and over again incessantly, giving him no choice but to pull his entire body away from her. He pried his hand out of her vice grip and got to his feet, practically running backward to the other side of the room. Mama May's upper body plopped down onto her table and lay there, limp. Purdue rubbed his hand, which still stung from the wound needed to initiate the vision. Part of him worried that Mama May was seriously hurt, or maybe even worse. She was just lying there, motionless. He remembered that she had been exhausted after seeing his future the first time but now it looked even worse.

Purdue walked over and slowly put a hand on

her shoulder, hoping to nudge her back to her senses. The moment his hand touched her shoulder, the frail woman sprang up and grabbed hold of his wrist. Purdue let out a yell but he was completely overpowered by the seer. She forced his hand back onto the table, rubbing his palm against it and smearing what was left of his blood in front of her. She barely seemed to even notice him. All he was to her in this state was an ink jar, providing the necessary material she needed to get her task done and write down the message that she felt obligated to provide. Her eyes were wide as she investigated the red stain in front of her.

"The world is not ready for what's to come. It's not ready. It never was. You will try to make it ready...you will try...but it will not matter. The cold will claim the ones who dare to feel it. The blades will find the backs that they mean to betray. And a sacrifice will be made in that temple. That sacrifice will change everything. Your future depends on that sacrifice. Your enemies depend on that sacrifice. And once it is made...it cannot be undone. It is a toll that must be paid for what you want most. And sacrifices are not easy...sacrifices are no easy...sacrifices are not easy..."

She wasn't shrieking this time. She seemed far too tired for that kind of reaction. Instead, she slowly continued to speak to herself, like the residual effects of what she saw were still leaving her body. Purdue made sure she didn't fall over or flop down on the table again but he was glad when he finally got his arm away. He wasn't going to get too close again, only for her to grab him once more. He didn't need to be startled that way again.

Purdue stuck around for a while longer, keeping an eye on Mama May to make sure she was okay. She looked exhausted and overwhelmed by all of the visions that she had found in the blood. Purdue wrapped up his hand and then cleaned off some of the blood on the table in front of Mama May. He didn't need her catching any more glimpses in those bloodstains and losing her mind again. As he wiped off some of his own blood, Mama May seemed to be regaining some of her senses.

"You will need to be careful out there, Mr. Purdue." He half-expected her to be looking at the few speckles of blood still left on the table but was surprised when she was looking at him with eyes that weren't wide or distant. She was looking at him wearily, and he could tell she was completely in the present. She was completely aware of her surroundings. "That is not a warning of vision. This is...just...I felt I needed to say about what might come. If what I saw is the path that you end up walking, then you have much to be cautious about."

"I will take everything you said into consideration."

Of course he would. How could he not? All of the things she told him were food for thought, and most of them didn't sound like anything pleasant. Most of them were cryptic and dread-inducing but he still tried to go over them in his head as he waited to make sure Mama May was going to be okay. He sat there, staring at the bandage wrapped around his hand and did his best to recollect every detail that she told him.

It was going to be cold—naturally. His objective was in the Arctic. That was to be expected and not at all a surprise. He didn't need a psychic to tell him that but at least it was something. He hadn't told Mama May where his destination was going to be so her knowing it would be cold just yet again proved the legitimacy of her abilities.

She spoke about the cold place being infested with evil that he had faced before. That sounded a whole lot like the Order of the Black Sun, especially when she went on to say that the dead man was still walking. Julian Corvus was a dead man at one point, however briefly, and he was absolutely still walking. When she'd elaborated, she made it sound like the whole world was going to be bowing to this dead man and that made Purdue more than slightly nervous. Did that mean Julian was going to win? Would he take over the world the second he got his wish? Would no one have any choice anymore but to bow to him?

Next...next...he struggled to remember. It was all so much to process. If it was too much for him to just hear about and try to remember, he couldn't imagine what it must have been like for Mama May, who had all of these possible futures practically downloaded directly into the lobes of her brain. It must have been so overwhelming...it clearly was, considering how it sapped the energy right out of her every time she saw any of his future.

There was something about a key and a cage. A key that unlocked the doors to a cage, but there was also a glass cage with darkness inside. And this was some sort of darkness that could see him and wanted to escape and shatter its prison. Hopefully he wouldn't have to be careful about unleashing some unspeakable darkness, but glass wasn't difficult to break most of the time. Maybe he would accidentally let something loose that he shouldn't...some sort of horrible Pandora's Box situation where he let something out that he wouldn't be able to put back in.

Then there was the other man. It didn't sound like the same man as the dead man but someone else entirely; someone standing on top of a darkened sun. That was one of the strangest of her prophecies of the night. He could understand the idea of freezing environments or even a dead man still walking but a man standing on top of a sun wasn't a usual sight at all. But the sun she described sounded an awful lot like the Black Sun, and if that was the case, then he shouldn't be so literal with the message. That man could be standing on top of the Black Sun...as in being above that infuriating secret society.

And then she had moved on to warning him about those blades stabbing people in the back.

Being stabbed in the back obviously meant betrayal, but the way she talked about, it sounded like it was going to happen to a lot of people. Whatever was coming next, it was going to inspire a whole lot of backstabbing. Purdue just had to hope that his back wouldn't be one of the ones that ended up with a blade in it. It might be more difficult than that though, if she was right about just how many people were going to end up pulling knives out of themselves.

And finally, there was all of her warnings about the sacrifice. That sacrifice that was needed to make a wish inside of the Mayan temple was something that he was already somewhat anxious about, but he had tried to put it out of his mind. After all, a sacrifice could mean a lot of different things...but the way she had said it made it very clear that it was going to be anything good. Based on her words, the sacrifice that needed to be made wasn't going to be an easy one, and it wasn't going to be one that he expected. For all he knew, he might end up being the one who was sacrificed. That was probably the one sacrifice Julian Corvus would perform if given the chance and the choice.

The cold. The dead man being bowed to. The glass cage with darkness inside. The man standing on the black sun. Blades piercing backs. And of course, the notion that sacrifices were not easy. All of those visions filled Purdue with an extreme sense of dread. Suddenly, things seemed bleaker than they had before, but he hadn't come to Mama

May's for good news. He came to hear anything that might be able to benefit him in the future. It was helpful to have even a vague idea of what you might be up against; good or bad news didn't matter, as long as it could be beneficial to know.

Mama May started to perk up and she shook her head at Purdue. "What are you still doing here, boy?"

"I'm just making sure you didn't croak," Purdue said with a wink. "I would feel guilty if you died from seeing my future. That would be on me, for having such a terrible fate waiting for me. I just would rather if you're going to die, let it be from natural causes or someone else's vision. Not mine."

"How gallant of you," Mama May said with a shake of her head. "I would like to be honest with you, Purdue. What I just saw...I don't know if it will happen but if it does, I don't expect you to get out of it all in one piece. Honestly, I would already be preparing your funeral arrangements if you hadn't surprised me before. The last time you came, your future looked very bad too...and yet you survived. Maybe...just maybe you can do it again."

"I don't intend to die, if that wasn't obvious," Purdue said. "At least not now. Who knows years down the road when I'm as old as you and unable to get out of bed...I might not have a choice then. But, I enjoy life far too much to just lay back and let this horrifying doom come to kill me. That's never been my way. I'm far too stubborn of a bastard, aye?"

"Yes," Mama May said, and even smiled. "I suppose you are. If you do see Jean-Luc...please get him to safety. I do not know if he still lives, but I have hope that he does. He is also stubborn, much like you, and this community is missing a large piece of our heart without him around. I've had to take measures to stop the city from clearing out his book shop but I don't know how much longer I'll be able to do it."

"If I can, you know I'll get him back. We didn't get a chance to work together long but he was a good guy. I'm sorry I got him wrapped up in all of this. The people that I'm up against...this wasn't Jean's fight. He should never have been caught in the middle."

"And that's why you're going to be the one to get him back," Mama May said firmly, like she was a mother scolding her son to improve his grades. "You got him into this mess. If he is alive, then you are going to get him back."

"Aye," Purdue said. "That's fair enough. I'll do my best."

Mama May seemed well enough to be by herself again. Purdue turned to leave, his head racing with thoughts. There were all of the visions that she described to him, and then there was the looming threat ahead of him, and the stakes that came with it. He had to stop the Order of the Black Sun for good, and if it was possible, he needed to save all of the friends he had lost.

Purdue left the fortune teller's house only to

find a very angry line of visitors waiting for him. He didn't realize how long his conversation with her had been but then again, he had stayed for a while after. They were probably used to going in, hearing a quick fortune or two and then leaving. Purdue ignored them. They were the least of his concerns and they would get over it. The things he really had to worry about were much more costly.

Now that he had an idea of what he might be facing, he had to go toward it, and the first step was meeting up with Sam. From there, it was going to be a direct journey to the Mayan temple that was waiting for them in the Arctic.

6

CHAPTER SIX – HEADS IN THE CLOUDS

Purdue and Sam met up shortly after Purdue's eventful conversation with Mama May. From there, they boarded a private jet that Purdue had been renting out and using for travel, buckling in as they took off. Once they were in the air, Purdue told Sam all about his talk with the fortune teller. He expected Sam to look wide eyed and fascinated by all of the visions but he couldn't have looked more distracted. He just kept staring out the window and looking at the fluffy clouds that they passed by.

By the time Purdue finished the story, Sam just nodded and gave him a polite and curt smile. His non-reaction was aggravating but Purdue tried to not let it piss him off too much.

When Sam finally spoke, it had nothing to do with Mama May's visions or the horrors that they might be flying toward.

"She's a really good girl, Purdue."

Despite Purdue opening up their talk with Mama May's visions, Sam had spent the majority of their journey so far ranting about his new girlfriend and Purdue was probably a few moments away from throwing himself from his own private plane. It was one thing to be dating someone or just seeing someone casually. It was fine to be very obviously infatuated with someone, but Sam seemed utterly obsessed. Whoever this girl was, she must have been quite the woman to turn Sam's otherwise hardened heart into complete mush. Seeing Sam this way was annoying enough, especially when he needed Sam's head focused on the mission ahead of them. He didn't invite him along just to hear gossip about his love live.

Sam hadn't even asked a single question about the Moving Temple of Ah Puch since boarding the private jet. Purdue had come with all sorts of answers prepared just to make sure that they were both on the same page, but they clearly weren't. They weren't even on different chapters. Sam was on an entirely different book than him—some horrid, sappy romance novella.

"Aye, sounds it. Too good if you ask me. Like the kind of lady who sounds like she came straight out of your imagination...and those are the ladies you need to watch out for the most, believe me. There's a reason imagination is imagination and dreams are dreams. They belong up here." He tapped his forehead. "Not staring you in the face and promising you paradise."

"She's real, Purdue, and she's wonderful. Kendra is smart, funny, gorgeous. She's one of those people that makes everyone else in the room feel good the second she walks in. It's magnetic almost. Like real actual attraction..."

Purdue stuck out his tongue. "Stop it, you bastard. Are you trying to make me sick? Like I said, she sounds too good to be true. That's my professional opinion. Take it or leave it."

"You are just being a downer," Sam said with a shake of his head. "A goddamn pessimist pissing on my happiness."

"On the contrary, I've spent every moment of my life being an optimist. Being a billionaire made that easy. The future was always full of hope when I could do whatever the hell I wanted whenever the hell I wanted to do it. But, after all of this shit happened, I've come to realize that it's a damn tiring thing to always be looking on the bright side. Sometimes you need to take a break and just tell the honest, brutal, horrible truth. And the truth is, you just met this lady not long ago, aye? Yet here you are, blabbering on about her like some lovesick moron. It's gross and I take personal offense to it."

Sam didn't look pleased with that response but after spending the last hour enduring that torturous talk, he really didn't care how Sam felt about it. He was lucky that Purdue hadn't shut him up forever ago.

It was nice that Purdue could afford a private jet again. He may not have been able to buy his own, but he could still rent one out with the money he did have. It was just still depressing that his previous private plane had been destroyed by the Order of the Black Sun when they took everything else too. Renting one was a downgrade, but it would work well enough. It made traveling much more efficient than it had been as of late. He had to be creative after his money was ripped away from him but ever since he found the treasure of the legendary pirate, Admiral Walton Ogden, things had been progressively improving again.

Hopefully, the Moving Temple of Ah Puch could help finish putting everything else back into place. That would be convenient and would save a whole lot of time, money, and most of all, effort. One successful venture now could save them from having to push their way through a dozen tougher ones in the future.

At least with this one, they weren't desperately searching for some hidden place. They knew exactly where the Moving Temple was. The only difficulty was that there was no way of knowing just how long that the temple was going to stay there.

“So what are we going to be wishing for in this temple exactly?” Sam asked awkwardly.

Neither of them could be sure that those legends were even true, but in the event that they were, they should have a plan. Purdue had given the question some thought. If everything he learned about the place was true – and, based on the fact that the legends about the temple transporting around were true - there was a decent chance that the other half of the story was true too. He had hopes that the altar really was going to be able to give them a wish in exchange for a sacrifice.

"I don't know how it exactly works obviously but if it does, then we need to wish for the Order of the Black Sun to be over and done with and to free Nina, Charles, and Jean."

"Really?" Sam asked, looking confused. "I was thinking I could wish for something nice for Kendra." Sam seemed even happier just from mentioning her name. Purdue made sure that he saw how annoyed he was by even proposing the idea. Sam just smiled. "I'm only joking. Relax."

"You better be."

"I think that's a good plan. It removes all of our problems at once. Wouldn't that be a wonderful thing? But the wish is exchanged for a sacrifice...what kind of sacrifice do you think we're looking at here potentially?"

"I don't imagine a lamb or a rabbit is going to do. It's probably going to have to be a human."

"And we're going to do that?"

"We may have some Black Sun volunteers, and some of them I'd hardly even consider human anymore, those crazy bastards. And, when you think about it, it might be worth it if it's all for a good cause."

"You sound like a sociopath," Sam said with a snort.

Purdue just chuckled and shrugged. "Maybe I

am. Forgive me for not having any sympathy for the bastards that took everything from me. They could all fall off a cliff and I wouldn't bat an eye. Death is honestly too easy for any of them."

"So you really think the Order of the Black Sun is going to be at the temple?"

"With this much media coverage, absolutely." Purdue was more certain of that than he was of anything else. He knew Julian Corvus and he knew that this was too good of an opportunity for him to pass up. "They already tried to use the temple to ambush me in Honduras. They'll see that it's moved and they'll set up another trap again. That's the kind of man Julian is."

"So why are we going in with just the two of us? Without any kind of back up?"

"You want to bring an army with us?"

"Not an army exactly but there are people who would probably help us. What about Aya and her crew? They were great when we had to get that pearl. Without them, the Wharf Man might have skinned us both."

"I'm aware," Purdue said. "But I didn't want to risk that. This isn't their fight. The Wharf Man was. They wanted to help bring him down and they owed me for helping them get away from his crime ring. They have nothing to do with the Order of the Black Sun. Why let them all potentially get killed doing something that they have no stake in. No. This is our fight, Sam. We have to put an end to it."

"Sure," Sam said. "I understand that. But...we

couldn't have at least brought along some mercenaries or something for some extra muscle? Give them a few dollars and it would be their fight too."

"Sam."

"You at least brought some artifacts to use, right? That pearl, for instance?"

"Aye," Purdue said and pointed at his bag. "Of course I did."

The two of them sat in uncomfortable silence for a bit. They soared toward their destination as the air outside naturally grew colder. They both knew the gravity of this particular quest. It was different than their usual searches for relics and lost civilizations. This was a personal journey that could change their lives forever. It could be the moment that turned their lives back around for good or it could be a final stand against an enemy that they couldn't beat.

Finally, Sam broke the silence, but not in the way that Purdue hoped for.

"You're going to love her."

Purdue groaned. "Will you shut yer yap already?"

7

CHAPTER SEVEN – THE ROGUE FLAME IN THE SUN

Elijah Dane walked toward Julian's quarters with some trepidation. Ever since he gave Nina the key to her cell, he was waiting for his world to crash down on him. It was a necessary risk but it put him in a vulnerable position. If anyone found out that he was conspiring against Julian, he would end up like Sasha—dead. And if Elijah was dead, all of those priceless relics in the deep vault probably wouldn't last long.

He entered the room, trying to ready himself for any and all reasons for Julian summoning him. He braced himself for the worst. He wished he was in the deep vault, behind those enormous reinforced doors and far away from danger.

As he walked in, he pushed his glasses up his nose and kept his composure. He couldn't let his stress be seen. Julian was sitting at his desk, looking pleased—which could be either good or bad for Elijah.

"I have news for you, Mr. Dane." Julian may have looked calm but his emotions were impossible to predict. He could go from elated to murderous in seconds. Elijah knew better than to feel comfortable around an erratic man like Julian Corvus. "Exciting news for you."

"Oh?" Elijah didn't even want to risk falling into some verbal trap that would confirm his treachery. He kept his responses short, letting Julian lead the conversation. If Julian knew the truth, he would have to drag Elijah into any sort of confession, because Elijah wasn't just going to admit to it easily.

"Yes," Julian said with some giddiness. "We know where Purdue is going next. We will descend on him in full force this time. They would completely overwhelm him. Then bury him."

Most people would have relaxed now that Julian wasn't coming even close to talking about betrayal or loyalty but Elijah knew better than that. He knew that Julian was the type of man who could say all of this, just to end up slitting a throat or two.

"Interesting..." Elijah said simply. He had to keep things neutral. "Perhaps we will be successful this time."

"We will," Julian said confidently. "He can't beat all of us."

"So why is this particularly exciting news for me?"

"Because when I say that we will go in full force, all of us, I mean all of us. You included. Are you ready for a field mission?"

Elijah wanted to shout in protest but kept his voice calm, but firm.

"When I joined, I was told that I wouldn't have to participate out there. My job was solely the care of the relics. I don't have much training in field work so I wouldn't be much use out there. That was the agreement, and the conditions of my recruitment after I had been this order's prisoner. I wouldn't have to take part in any of the things the rest of you do--"

Julian's lips formed a thin smile and his gray eyes narrowed like a snake's. "Things change."

Elijah wanted to argue but there was no point fighting the decision. Julian Corvus was the leader of the order. His word was law within the society. Resisting his commands too much would only arouse suspicion. If Elijah wanted to survive, he had to retain his loyal image at all costs.

"And where are we going on this field mission?" Elijah tried his best not to sound bitter but it was difficult. He was more than a little annoyed by being forced into doing the grunt work. He was never supposed to be a soldier on the front lines. He didn't have the stomach for it. He decided to tack on another question that would at least partially put him back on Julian's good side. "Where will David Purdue's burial site be?"

“You have seen the news of the Mayan temple in the Arctic, yes?”

“I have not,” Elijah said honestly but it did sound curious. “I tend not to pay too much attention to current events. So many of them turn out to be insignificant or pointless. Very few have any real bearing on the future.”

“This one will. The temple spontaneously appeared up there just days ago.” Julian rummaged through a folder and put two large pictures on the table top. “Satellite imaging captured these pictures milliseconds apart.”

The image on the left showed a bird's eye view of a vast icy terrain, nothing more than a sheet of white like a blank canvas waiting to be bathed in paint. The picture on the right would have been identical if not for a large dark shape that was in the center of the image, a blemish on the once clear canvas of snow.

Elijah looked at the time stamps just to be certain. Sure enough, the pictures were taken a millisecond apart. That whole structure popped into existence instantaneously. It shouldn't have been possible, yet there it was. As impossible as the immortal man stranding across from him. Since becoming part of the Order of the Black Sun, Elijah had learned that anything once thought to be impossible could very easily be entirely possible.

“Strange, isn't it?” Julian asked, staring at Elijah as he looked at the pictures.

Julian used that tactic to keep his people in line. He would do nothing but watch them react to something, to figure out exactly what buttons to push when he needed to.

"Quite strange, yes." Elijah was once again short with his answers.

"Purdue is going there and so shall we. As our most knowledgeable historian, I want you to find out what you can about that place. And who knows...we might find all kinds of interesting relics there to dust off."

Even that potential wasn't enough to excite Elijah.

He couldn't help but feel a field mission meant death for an introvert like him.

SOON AFTER, Julian gathered most of the operatives that were present in the facility into one room to be briefed about their next mission. Usually, the operatives broke into small teams—usually duos or teams of three—to spread their influence throughout the world, but this was going to be different. This was the first time he had assembled so many at once since they had invaded David Purdue's home and burned it down. He loved seeing so many of his underlings in one place. It made him feel powerful, like he was the general at the head of an army.

Julian explained the situation to them and everyone stared at him in disbelief once he got to the parts about the teleporting temple and the altar inside that could grant someone any wish. It was a hard pill for some to swallow but he made sure that he shoved that idea right down their throats until they accepted it. By the end of his presentation, many still looked bewildered but there were a few that at least looked intrigued. Especially once he brought up his endgame.

"My hope is that the stories about this altar are true. With it, we could take this world by force."

"What do you mean? What would we wish for?" Someone called out.

Julian's gray eyes scanned the crowd of faces, almost like he was looking for the culprit who heckled him. After a moment of intimidation, he answered the question.

"We would wish for complete control, of course. That this world would have no choice but to bow before us. Just like they should. Perhaps someday they will if we keep playing things smart, but this would accelerate the process. We could make the changes we want far sooner than we ever would have been able to."

A lot of the spectators nodded in approval to this plan. They wanted to be recognized for their greatness; they wanted the Order of the Black Sun to stop being some shadow organization that had to maneuver stealthily around the world. Things operating that way didn't give them the chance for much glory. They were trying to make a better world but would never, ever be recognized for this efforts. Perhaps with a wish and the power that came from it, they would be able to finally shine the Black Sun's light on the rest of the world.

"Not to mention..." Julian said carefully. "When this temple was in Honduras, David Purdue went there."

There was quiet chatter among the Black Sun and some of them didn't look pleased by the direction the conversation was going. Julian's feud with the order's greatest enemy had initially been something they admired about him. His first act as leader was proclaiming that he was going to eliminate Purdue from ever being a problem for them ever again. And he had initially seemed to honor that pledge, but it turned out Purdue had survived the attack. Since then, they were all a bit more skeptical about how effective he could be against the explorer.

Purdue could sense the negativity brewing in the crowd and was quick to start speaking again, hoping to recover their support. "Mr. Purdue will come back to the temple, no matter where it is. It has already been broadcast all over the news. By now he must know where the temple ended up. He will come and we will be waiting for him. We will confront him and settle the fighting between us once and for all. We could even use him as the sacrifice to initiate the wish. I can't be the only one that wants to bleed him out on the sacrificial altar."

There were nervous glances among the Black Sun members. They were all well aware of Julian's sadism by this point. They had all just hoped that this new plan of his had nothing to do with his vendetta against David Purdue. Enemy or not, they knew that the plan shouldn't rely on him showing up to face them. So many of Julian's decisions since becoming leader were dictated by that feud.

"This is our chance to finish him. For good this time. We've already set traps for him all over the world. Think of this as just another one of those...but on a much larger scale. We can end this war that he wants with us before it even begins."

Galen Fitzgerald shakily rose to his feet, putting his weight on his walking stick. The Irishman didn't look pleased by what he was hearing. He was shaking his head, like he was trying to shake bad ideas out of his brain.

"So this isn't just about making a wish that could give us everything? It should be, shouldn't it? No, instead you are talking about a war that we don't need to fight, eh? This war we're getting into...it's all just to kill Davy...he's one man. He's a bastard of a man but still...just a man."

There were murmurs of agreement among the spectators.

Julian didn't mind. Galen was a fool and if he needed to put him in his place, then he would.

"Get to the point, Galen. I'm not in the mood to

listen to you tiptoe around whatever it is that you're actually trying to say."

Galen hated how Julian spoke down to him but he carried on anyway. "All I am saying...is why make this much trouble for one guy? I will go kill him myself. I know Oniel would too--"

Oniel, the mute assassin that was only recently recruited after years of working for the Wharf Man's crime ring, gave a firm nod of his head beside them. He was a scary figure even among the Black Sun members, but he had been a close ally of Julian's ever since his recruitment. They were both relatively new to the Order of the Black Sun and stuck together most of the time.

Julian cut him off. "What a novel idea, Mr. Fitzgerald. Send a few men to handle him quietly. Truly a genius strategy. Unheard of. Perhaps you haven't noticed but we tried taking that path. Our top enforcers gave it their shot, and it didn't work. Victor and Vincent Moore, Torsten, Clive...they all tried their hands and they all failed—even after we armed them with some of history's most dangerous weapons. David Purdue still survived. Then I tried to kill himself but even then...he endured and he is still out there."

Julian realized he was opening himself up for criticism. Galen could jump on the fact that Julian couldn't finish Purdue himself, but the Irishman didn't try and utilize that opening. He probably didn't have the stones to call him out like that.

"But he only survived because of that Templar

sword, right? And Sasha helping him. He won't have either of those things anymore. So we can--"

"We're trying something else," Julian snapped, not wanting to hear anymore. "I have already decided. You want your shot at him. I understand that but tell me...what chance against him does a cripple with little combat experience have compared to the highly trained kill squad that we already threw at him?"

"I know Davy. I know his--"

"No. That's not good enough. The time for handling this quietly is over. If we want to the Order of the Black Sun to be free of the blight that is David Purdue, then we need to descend on him in force. Erase him for good. This is our chance to do it right. To rectify the mistakes that were made. There won't be any more mishaps. We won't even risk them this time."

"But--"

"That is my final decision. Perhaps you can take a shot at him when we sweep over him. I can't promise that there will be much of him but you're welcome to take a swing, or pick at whatever scraps are left when we're done."

Galen's face was dark red. He looked like a child who was being ignored by his parents despite all of his efforts to win their attention. He was practically dancing on top of a moving car, screaming for them to look at him. He wasn't getting any of the validation he was hoping for In fact, all he was getting was scorn.

There was some laughter from the fellow members of the order but Galen just glowered at anyone that was chuckling. He gave one last hateful glance at Julian before sitting back down in his seat.

Luckily, that moment of mutiny passed quickly and Julian felt like he was back in control of the room again. He would punish Galen for that insubordination at some point, but for now, he needed every member of the Black Sun to be united against Purdue. As much as Galen may have scoffed at the idea of a final battle against Purdue, it was exactly what Julian wanted.

It was too perfect. Who better to grant him his immortality than Purdue. He could kill him on the altar, make him his sacrifice, and then gain the godhood that he had in mind. And if the stories about the temple were incorrect, then at least Purdue would have died in a fashion that Julian could appreciate. He would be satisfied either way.

The Order of the Black Sun would just have to accept it.

Their satisfaction didn't really matter to him.

ELIJAH DANE COULD FEEL the change that was happening within the group. Things in the Order of the Black Sun had only grown more intense since they learned about David Purdue's survival and the failed attempts to put him down for good. While Julian Corvus was an intimidating force, he was proving that he wasn't nearly as efficient as they all believed when he first made his claim for leadership. All of his posturing about ending Purdue hadn't amounted to anything of real substance. Despite all of his threats and the fear he inspired, Julian was just as ineffective as the old leadership had been. But no one would ever voice thoughts like that aloud. At least, that's how it used to be. But the cracks were starting to show, and he wasn't the only one noticing. It would start with someone like Galen Fitzgerald, someone easily angered and who wasn't afraid to loudly give his controversial opinions. He would speak his mind enough to get others thinking and soon enough, there would be dissention within the ranks.

There was a time when Elijah would have done his best to nip a revolt like that in the bud. But now, after deciding that Julian wasn't the leader he wanted to follow, he wouldn't do anything to try and contain that brewing spark of rebellion. No, if anything, Elijah would do all he could to fan the flames until the Order of the Black Sun burst into an inferno of resistance against their leader. A swift mutiny would be nice, but he would settle for an internal civil war if it came down to it.

Elijah didn't enjoy talking to Galen. He was an unpleasant, arrogant jerk that spent all of his conversations patting himself on the back. He was a narcissist and a prick but he was the perfect person to start openly questioning Julian's commands.

And he was petty enough to hold even the smallest grudge and let it fester into full blown disdain.

While most of the operatives filed out of the room, Elijah approached Galen and kept his voice low. "Quite the meeting, Galen."

The Irishman looked surprised that Elijah was even speaking to him. Usually their conversations were reserved for the brief moments that Galen would drop off artifacts that he had collected to the deep vaults for Elijah to tend to. Those chats weren't long and were usually just small talk. Mostly, it was Galen just bragging about how he had managed to obtain the relic he was delivering and Elijah spent most of the time trying to restrain himself from throttling the smug Irish bastard.

"Aye, quite the meeting indeed. Can you believe this? Even with this temple up for grabs, our fearless leader is still fixated on Purdue. I hate Purdue too, we all know this, but--"

"You want to kill him yourself," Elijah said, adjusting his glasses. Galen wasn't a complicated man and he was very easy to read. There was nothing mysterious or ambiguous about him. He wasn't upset that Julian was too focused on Purdue for the sake of the order. He was upset because he didn't want Julian to get to Purdue first. "He humiliated you. I understand why you would want his head."

Galen looked taken aback but then clicked his tongue. "So what if I do? I deserve it more than Julian, don't I? He had his shot. He missed. Purdue is still alive because he had to make a big scene of it all. I would have bashed Purdue's head in until there was no way he was ever coming back from it. That's what I would still do...but somehow we're still following his lead, eh?"

"Of course we're following his lead," Elijah said with a bored yawn. "Leading is what leaders do. And he is the current leader of the order."

Galen lowered his voice to being barely above a whisper. "Maybe he shouldn't be."

"Maybe not," Elijah said, knowing that Galen was following his verbal breadcrumbs straight to the conclusions that he wanted him to make. If he wanted to turn some of the Black Sun against their sadistic leader, then Galen was the perfect one to target first, and this was proof of that. "And what do you intend to do about it?"

"Whatever I have to, eh?" Galen muttered with a crooked smile. "If a good opportunity ever presents itself, I will make sure I grab it with both hands and not let it go to waste."

Elijah nodded, acting like he was enthralled by Galen's notions. "I must say, I'm impressed, Galen. You clearly have a dizzying intellect."

That was how to get Galen Fitzgerald on your side. You just had to feed the Irishman some compliments and then he would love you forever. He was a petulant and sometimes dangerous force, but he could be very easy to manipulate once he was buttered up a little.

"I joined the Order of the Black Sun to try

something new," Galen explained, suddenly looking very serious. "But the most important thing to me has always been...well...me. That hasn't changed, eh? When it comes down to it, I don't care what Julian says. He doesn't control me."

Elijah cleaned off his glasses, feeling victorious. "You're right. He doesn't."

8

CHAPTER EIGHT – SEEING CLEARLY

Elijah barely knew what to even pack for this trip. He was so used to just being able to stick to the facility and the few rooms he traveled throughout it; his bedroom, the hallways, the deep vault, and even the kitchen on occasions when his growling stomach gave him no other choice than to give in and take a break. They were traveling north so he knew enough to pack warm but as far as the specifics, he was at a loss.

Elijah was completely useless with firearms. He would be lucky if he didn't blow off his own head or one of his own teammates' once he had a gun in his hand. He still couldn't fathom why he was being dragged into the field. It must have been a matter of numbers, which didn't make him feel any better. His knowledge and talents with curating the artifacts the order collected made him far too valuable of an asset to just put on the front lines.

Why would Julian risk letting Elijah get killed?

Did Julian already suspect that Elijah may not have been entirely loyal to him anymore? If so, what had given him away? He couldn't think of anything that he might have done. He'd been so cautious, especially when he was around any of the Black Sun. Or perhaps Julian didn't really care about the artifacts that the Black Sun collected...that seemed more likely. Julian seemed to prefer the hunt, rather than actually finding and taking the artifacts.

He turned to find Julian standing in his doorway. It took all of his strength not to scream and cower in the corner. Maybe Julian did know after all, and if he did...then he would make sure that Elijah was given a slow, painful death that would probably last years.

Julian's cold gray eyes scanned the room and stopped on the bag that Elijah was packing. He clapped his hands together once and stepped into the room, flashing a twisted smirk that didn't have any sort of real friendship behind it.

Elijah didn't know how he would defend himself if this got ugly, but he would do his best. His best wouldn't be enough though, he was fine admitting that. Julian was a trained killer that had once been the Black Sun's top enforcer, he had even been penalized for being too brutal with their targets. If they fought, Elijah would be killed. It was as simple as that. No matter what advantage he had, it wouldn't be enough. Then there was the matter of Julian's immortality, and that just sealed the deal. There was no way to win against an opponent like that.

"I've been giving it some thought, Mr. Dane. Perhaps it would be best to leave you behind. I would not put it past David Purdue to try and use this as an opportunity to try and come in here, to take back what we won from him. You are the guardian of all of those items in the deep vault. So maybe it's for the best that you stay that way and remain to protect our prizes from any possible thieves."

Elijah's nervousness eased up a little. He wanted to be happy about the decision. He knew that he would be useless out in the field and would likely be killed out there if he went. This was what he originally wanted to happen but after learning the details about Julian's plans, part of him wanted to be close to the action. If he was near to where everything was happening then maybe he could even sabotage Julian's efforts before it was too late. Staying behind now meant that he wouldn't have that chance. He couldn't exactly stop Julian from his desk in the deep vault.

"You will have a small crew to keep you company and to help keep watch. I'm not expecting trouble, but I would prefer to be overly cautious rather than to put all of my eggs into one basket. I would hate to have them all crack apart at once."

"I understand," Elijah said, trying not to look conflicted. He forced a tight little smirk. "That makes sense."

"Yes, it does."

Julian may not have been expecting trouble but that didn't mean it wouldn't come, even from within. No, Purdue probably wouldn't be coming to visit since he didn't even know where the Order of the Black Sun's facility was located. But plenty of Purdue's friends were inside and Elijah had already given one of them a key to freedom.

In fact, this Mayan temple may have given them all the perfect chance for a jail break.

ONCE ALL OF the helicopters departed, flying north toward the mysterious Mayan temple, Elijah immediately went down to the order's holding cells, straight to Nina Gould's cell. He was glad that she was still there. She must have been tempted to use that key and escape earlier but he was thankful that she didn't. Any earlier would have just gotten her caught; and leaving any later they might risk the majority of the Black Sun returning to base or even the after effects of whatever wish Julian was planning on making at the temple. This was the only perfect time to unlock her cell and make a break for it.

"It's time," he said. "The majority of the order is off on a mission. Julian, Boris, Galen...they're all gone. This is our chance to get the hell out of here."

Nina looked happy but nervous. "And go where?"

This mission they're on...it could end up giving Julian complete control over everything...and we don't want that, do we? Not to mention...your friend David Purdue might be there as well."

He didn't need to say anything else. Nina was reinvigorated and shot up to her feet just from hearing Purdue's name. She picked up the cell key from where she had hidden it on the floor. If it meant stopping Julian and helping Purdue, then she was very clearly willing to get moving. It was the only proof she needed to confirm that it was the best tie to break free from the chains she had been bound in for far too long.

Nina reached her arm through the bars and used the key to open the door to her cell. "What are we waiting for? Come on!"

From there, they went directly to Charles and Jean's cells, letting them loose. Both men were very suspicious of Elijah and he couldn't really blame them. The last time the three of them tried to escape, Elijah was the one to turn them back over to their Black Sun captors. They wouldn't be smart to completely trust him again—but they would see that he was sincere this time. Before, he was still loyal to the Order of the Black Sun but in the short time since then, Nina had opened his eyes to the truth. He was on the wrong side and was nothing more than a tool for the Black Sun to use.

There was nothing more that Elijah cared about than the artifacts inside of the deep vault, the precious and priceless items that were under his care. He had watched the Order of the Black Sun misuse them time and time again. They didn't care about the things they collected. All they saw was an arsenal of weapons or things they could use for leverage. That went against everything Elijah stood for and he wanted it to end. If he had enough hands, he would empty the deep vault of everything inside and snatch it from the Black Sun. They didn't deserve those artifacts, but unfortunately, he would have to leave them behind. Unless...Purdue came out on top and brought down the order. Then maybe there was still a chance he salvage those relics that he had worked so hard to maintain and keep safe.

Not to mention all of the horrors he had seen Julian commit as the leader.

He knew he was on the right team this time. He could feel it.

"What's happening?" Charles asked, glancing around nervously. Of course he would be on edge. During their failed escape, the former butler was killed and then revived by the Spear of Destiny, giving him immortality. Julian had used him as a lab rat, and since then, kept Charles in a hole where his immortality wouldn't make a difference except to drastically prolong his suffering. Julian enjoyed being powerful, and he couldn't stand the idea of someone that shared his power walking around. If anyone was going to be his equal, he would do his best to change that, even stuffing an old man into darkness for eternity.

These people didn't have to trust him. He'd done nothing but help the monsters that kept them in cages for months, that had upended their lives and taken away their freedoms. But, whether they liked it or not, they were all on the same side now. Julian Corvus had to be stopped.

"We're getting out of here."

Elijah led the three prisoners down the halls, carefully peeking around each and every corner they came to just to be safe. So far, they had managed to avoid any obstacles. The less messy of an escape, the better. But that luck wasn't meant to last apparently.

"Elijah?"

The young guard that approached was a fairly new recruit named Marco. He was distinguished from the rest of the new blood by the spiky dyed blond hair on top of his head. He was a broad-shouldered man but wasn't overly intelligent. Like far too many of the new Black Sun members, he was recruited for his muscles and his talent for causing harm rather than for his brains. That was Julian Corvus' Order of the Black Sun—a group that valued strength over knowledge.

The young guard looked from Elijah to the others, his eyes narrowing. "What's going on here exactly?"

Elijah could feel Jean and Charles' suspicious gazes searing into the back of his skull. This was probably the moment that they expected him to hand them over, but he didn't intend to do any such thing; not this time. He was going to make up for his mistakes and choose the right side of the line to stand on. And that meant being able to stand up to those who were on the other side of that battle line, even if they were once people he considered allies.

But, if he could get out of this without violence, that would still be best. The best course of action was to use his status, throw the weight he had within the order around a bit. He may have been a burly grunt of a man, but Marco was still new and could probably be rattled quite easily.

"That's none of your concern, Marco. You were assigned to help me keep this place secure."

Marco's eyes flicked from Elijah to the prisoners again, not seeming very convinced.

Elijah continued, "But if you really must know, Julian contacted me. He has decided that he would like to bring the prisoners to the temple. So that's what I'm going to do. You're welcome to try and hold me up some more but delays aren't appreciated within this order."

Marco stared hard at him with those beady eyes of his. His brain was obviously working hard to make sense of what he was hearing, but unfortunately, his brain wasn't nearly as strong as the rest of him was.

Still, he had that hesitation that most rookies working at a new job had. He didn't want to make a mistake and didn't want to make a tough decision by himself. He wanted guidance and reassurance from a superior.

Marco smacked his lips nervously and said, "Okay, let me just confirm it."

"Don't you trust me?" Elijah asked.

Marco stuttered uncomfortably and cleared his throat. He straightened his posture trying to look as confident in his response as possible. "It's not that. It's just a precaution. For security. Verification. You understand, yeah? We all got to do our jobs right, don't we?"

"Of course," Elijah said with a faked chuckle. "I'm only testing you. Go on. Julian can confirm it...though I'm not sure he will for a guppy like you. And you might be interrupting something important going on over there..."

Marco let out a nervous laugh and reached for his radio, but still stared at the prisoners cautiously. If he made contact with Julian, then the whole plan would be exposed. Elijah would be outed as a traitor and there was good chance none of them would ever have another chance to make it out of that hellhole again.

The second that he clicked down on the button to speak, Elijah threw as hard of a punch as he could muster. He wasn't a fighter at all and wasn't good in a brawl. Marco, on the other hand, was a well-trained soldier. If it turned into an actual scuffle, Elijah wouldn't stand much of a chance at all. Hopefully, Nina, Jean, or even Charles would hop in to help in time.

Thankfully, Elijah's punch crashed against Marco's face with enough force to knock him out cold. A sucker punch may not have been the honorable way to win, but it was still a win.

The young guard crumbled to the floor in a heap, limp and unconscious. When Elijah turned to check on his trio of escapees, they all looked at him with a mixture of surprise and admiration. That one punch might have just proven that his claims of having changed might actually be true. They dragged Marco down to the cells and locked him in the cage that they had been keeping Nina in. It felt like justice, even if Marco hadn't tormented her personally. Now he would at least know what it felt being on the other side of those bars.

Once they had him out of the way and difficult for anyone to just come across, they made their way back through the facility toward the exit. Elijah knew that there were at least fifteen operatives still stationed around the base—hardly anything more than a skeleton crew but still over three times as many people as they had. All they needed to do was get to the helicopters and take off. If they could do that without another incident, or delay, that might be able to catch up to Julian and the others.

It took even more caution than before, but Elijah led them to the Black Sun's private hanger that housed all of the helicopters. As they walked out and admired the half dozen vehicles ready to be commandeered, Elijah took a brief second to appreciate what was happening. This was it—the time to bring down the Order of the Black Sun for good.

It wasn't just Nina Gould's escape. It wasn't just Charles's escape. It wasn't even just Jean-Luc Gerard's escape. He had been a prisoner of the Black Sun too for a long time, longer than any of them even. He just was able to make the most of it, make his chains a little less visible. He could dress up and get to work, pretend that it was just his job rather than the servitude that he was forced into.

He pushed his glasses up the ridge of his nose. Lately, he had been seeing much more clearly than usual. He was seeing a whole new world than he had been. Now it was time to share what he saw with everyone else.

They all filed into the helicopter and the propeller above began its rotation, spinning to life. Soon enough, the headquarters for the Order of the Black Sun was behind them.

Elijah Dane was finally free, and now it was time for some payback.

9

CHAPTER NINE – THE NORTHERN LIGHTS

Galen felt like he belonged in the lead chopper with Julian but was constantly relegated to the last helicopter in line. He sat as he always did, beside Oniel, who had become his most frequent partner on expeditions. He appreciated his partner's silence thanks to his missing tongue, as he could just bounce ideas off of him without having to hear any sort of verbal reprisal. Oniel also had plenty of experience in killing thanks to his time as part of a notorious Jamaican crime ring, so he helped make Galen a little more dangerous simply by association. He also shared his desire to murder David Purdue and his disdain for how Julian led the order.

"This is shit," Galen said, staring out the window at the white ground beneath them. "If he wasn't going to let us go after Davy then he should have at least let us take point on this expedition to that Mayan temple. I've been all over the world, gone to plenty of old places. I know the architecture well. I could be a lot more help if he utilized me. He obviously never bothered to read my bloody books, eh? He'd know just how much great shit I've accomplished if he did. Hell, he could just read the back cover and see for himself. It's a load of shit."

Oniel remained as quiet as always beside him. He'd grown used to Galen's almost constant posturing and complaining.

"He sent everybody but us after Davy when you and I know him best. I've known him for years. Went on that expedition for the Spear of Destiny some time ago. And you were on that boat with him, looking for that pirate's gold. You and I know him far better than Julian, yet Julian is sending out a bunch of a poor bastards who don't know the first thing about how annoying David Purdue can be. That's just bad planning and bad leadership."

As much as he wanted to scream all of this to the heavens, Galen kept his voice low. There were plenty of people in the order and on that plane that supported Julian Corvus. He wasn't a very popular leader but he had a small group of devoted followers—morons—who just probably wanted to earn favor to rise higher in the order.

Galen didn't like kissing other people's asses. Most people didn't deserve it. If anyone deserved more ass kisses than he got, it was him.

"We should be out there hunting that smug

bastard down before he comes and interrupts more of the order's plans. That should be the priority. Instead, we're relying on some new girl's information that Purdue is going to this temple...but we can't know that for sure. This could all be a goddamn waste of all of our time."

Oniel gave a simple few nods of his head in agreement. Even if he could speak, he still wouldn't be able to speak nearly as much as Galen could. It was physically impossible for anyone else to be able to talk as much as he did. No one else had a big enough ego.

THE HELICOPTERS LANDED, forming a large perimeter around the temple. As the Black Sun operatives poured out and gathered around, Galen was sure to be standing near Julian. He wanted to hear the plan, and he wanted to remind everyone that he was important and close to the inner workings. Most of all, he wanted to show Julian that he belonged in that lead helicopter and not left to rot at the back of the pack.

Julian explained the plan thoroughly, making sure that he wasn't skipping any of the finer details. "We'll enter the temple in teams of six, each dispersed throughout. We will set up lighting and many will map out a grid of the entire place."

"Excuse me," Galen interjected.

Many of the others gathered around looked at him with some bewilderment, baffled that he would dare to interrupt their great and powerful leader. Galen didn't care who he was talking over, especially not someone like Julian Corvus. The others let their shock show but Julian didn't even look at him. He just stared at the snowy ground with some annoyance, but didn't even offer him the slightest bit of attention.

Galen ignored the slight, putting it in a mental pocket to be pissed off about later. “All I'm saying is that that temple right there up and vanished. Poof. Went from a bloody to jungle to this Christmas wasteland, and we're all supposed to take our sweet time in there? What if it moves again with all of us inside? Who knows if we can even survive that?”

Julian scoffed but still didn't look at him.

“I'm just trying to be cautious, eh? Shouldn't we all be?”

“What exactly are you suggesting, Mr. Fitzgerald?” Julian said coldly. “Is this something that you came up with for that book of yours? Forgive me, I never had a chance to read it. No, you have your orders. I have given them. My plan is the only plan. Understood?”

Galen wanted to bash Julian over the head with his walking stick, beat him to death for talking down to him like that in front of everyone. It was always the same. He went ignored because he wasn't considered part of the inner circle, not really.

But if he didn't do as he was told, he knew that Julian wouldn't hesitate to excommunicate him from the Black Sun or do something much, much worse.

"Understood," Galen said, biting his tongue.

As they made their way across the patch of ice between the helicopters and the temple, Galen noticed that Julian was carrying the Spear of Destiny in one of his hands. He recognized it immediately. After all, Galen had spent quite a lot of time trying to acquire that spear. He would have gotten it too if he wasn't caught in the middle of David Purdue's and Julian Corvus's tug of war. That was another thing that Galen deserved that Julian had taken from him.

"Why bring the spear?" Galen asked.

Julian looked like he was tempted to ignore him again but then answered. "A precaution. If some of us die, I would rather have this than a defibrillator wouldn't you? And if this is the day when we claim true victory over the world, I want this with me."

It seemed unnecessary but Galen kept that thought to himself. He had already pissed off Julian enough. He would love to upset him some more but he knew that Julian wasn't the most stable person. If he pushed him a little too far, Galen may end up with a bullet between his eyes. And he highly doubted Julian would ever use the Spear of Destiny to revive him.

The teams entered the temple, all bearing flashlights and lighting fixtures to light the entire inside of it up. There was no point exploring the temple if no one could see anything. Galen begrudgingly accepted going in with the last group inside. It was tough to keep up with some of his teammates due to his limp, but he did his best. He didn't want to be left behind by anyone, let alone Julian Corvus. Of course he was the first to enter. That bastard wanted to see everything and take everything for himself.

The rest of the teams were probably already through the entire temple by the time Galen had just set his first few steps inside. It wasn't fair that they all had two working legs and weren't assigned to the back of the line. He deserved more respect than this. All he could do was hope that he found something that everyone else ahead of him was missing. That would show all of them that he wasn't baggage that they could just drag around. He had done more exploring around the world than most of them probably. He was a well-respected and well known purveyor of all kinds of artifacts. He was more capable than most of them, despite what the feedback for his autobiography had said. They all just didn't want him to overshadow them.

One of the only benefits to being the last inside was that the place was already most lit up thanks to the efforts of everyone in front of him. It gave him a good look at all of the cracked and worn walls of the temple around him. He could hear voices down the corridors. His own team had already broken away ahead of him. Everyone else was hard at work but he had barely begun.

"Galen?"

The voice that spoke his name was hoarse and when he turned around, he almost expected to see some kind of creature—but it was a bald man that he recognized—Lucius. He was filthy, and pale, keeping close to the stone walls as he slowly crept toward Galen.

"Galen, is that you?"

He was blinking hard, probably trying to get his eyes readjusted to the light. He had been stuck in this dark place for weeks. He didn't have much hope of escape either, considering that all there was outside but a barren frozen landscape that he would never survive. If the cold didn't get him, then he would starve to death.

"Lucius...looks like you've had a rough go of it, eh? Last I heard, you were in Honduras..."

"I was," Lucius said quietly. His voice was shaky and his voice so raspy. He obviously hadn't been getting enough food or water in this place. "I was, yes. I was. Me and Charlotte. Where—where is she?"

"No one knows," Galen said. "She was with you."

"She was guarding...guarding outside but then that asshole got away and this place moved. It all happened so fast. Too fast. Yes, far too fast."

"Who got away?"

"David Purdue. We had him, Galen. I swear we

had him. I swear. But...but he slipped by us. We would have killed him this place just..." He held out his hands, pointing his fingers at the floor. "If this place had just stayed put like it should have...how did it....how did it move, Galen?"

"Hell if I know."

"How did it move!?" His yell was something of a roar at this point. "How did it move!?"

The scream was echoing through the temple. It wouldn't take long for the other teams to come running to investigate the disturbance. That might not be a bad thing, though. They would all see that Galen had actually found something while the rest of them were all still most likely roaming around empty handed.

"Just relax, eh?" Galen said but turned and shouted down the halls. "Oi! I found something!"

"I stepped outside and it was so cold. So cold...there was ice everywhere. It was hot before. Humid. There were trees. Trees that were on the ground. And Purdue was there...he was there...Charlotte...where is she?"

Lucius' ramblings were growing more incoherent. His time stuck up here had done a number on him. What he needed was some food, some drink, and some rest to at least start to screw his head back on straight. It must have been difficult being stuck in a place you didn't know, thinking that you were just going to slowly die.

"Where, Galen...where?"

There were footsteps hurrying down the

narrow stone hallways and voices calling to one another. A number of the Black Sun operatives came to Galen, looking pessimistic that he actually had anything of value but when he pointed his cane at Lucius, many of those doubtful faces filled with genuine shock.

"Is that Lucius?" one asked.

"Holy shit, it is!" said another.

"He's alive? Thought he died on that mission with Charlotte."

Lucius covered his face with his arms to avoid the glares of their flashlights, cowering away from the light after spending so long in the darkness. He had resigned himself to that darkness, knowing that the temple wasn't exactly accommodating but was at least protect him from the harsh conditions outside. He reminded Galen of a possum or some other nocturnal creature that wanted nothing to do with the daylight.

Julian pushed his way through the crowd of amazed Black Sun agents and even he looked startled by the sight of Lucius. He stormed over to him and grabbed his face. Despite Lucius' trembling and panic, Julian squeezed hard and examined him closely.

"So this is where you ended up, is it?"

"Please—please, please Julian. Don't. I didn't mean...I didn't mean...nothing went as it should have. None of it. It all went so wrong. So wrong. Purdue--"

"He bested you, yes," Julian said coldly. "I'm

very aware. I gave you a job to do and you failed at it. Completely and utterly blew your chance to earn your place in the inner circle."

Lucius was on the verge of tears but it was hard to tell if it was from being afraid or simply his eyes being irritated by the sudden influx of light into his life. But the more Julian spoke to him, the more terror filled his face. This Mayan temple might have driven him to starvation and madness, but he remembered Julian very well. No amount of time or hysteria could make him forget how terrified he was of the Black Sun's leader. That fear seemed to stitch up some of his nerves, able to form coherent sentences again.

"I didn't mean to. I didn't."

"Where is Charlotte?" Julian asked, ignoring Lucius' tearful pleas.

"I don't know. She was outside when Purdue escaped. I don't—"

"Shhhh, hush now," Julian said but it wasn't soothing or comforting at all. It was undeniably an order. Lucius struggled to comply, but he did, and held back more waterworks. Julian squeezed his face harder. "Purdue is most likely going to be on his way. You will have another chance. You won't fail me again." Lucius was still trembling like a spooked animal and Julian's commands weren't helping. "But...for now, we're going to get you cleaned up a bit. There's some spare clothes in one of the choppers. And we have water and rations.

We'll get your strength back up enough to get back at Purdue for leaving you in this place."

Lucius managed a shivering nod and he forced a yellow smile. Still, as he was taken away, he looked far from relaxed. Even Galen hoped that with some food in his stomach and some clean clothes that Lucius might get his head screwed back on straight. He doubted it. This place had done a number on him, but how could it not? It was a musty ancient temple that just reeked of death from the sacrifices performed there. It may have provided him some form of shelter from the icy weather outside, but it hadn't been a home to Lucius—for all he knew, it was going to be his tomb. And it would have been if the order hadn't come. He wouldn't have lasted much longer.

Galen glanced to Julian, waiting for him to thank him for finding Lucius but, as per usual, Julian barely noticed Galen standing beside him. He wasn't going to get any congratulations or any gratitude. If anything, Julian probably just thought of all of this as a distraction from whatever he was doing on the other end of the temple.

Without a word, Julian started walking back from the direction he came from. Some of the other agents followed suit and Galen followed them, hobbling behind them. Oniel walked beside him but he barely ever noticed him. It wasn't just that he didn't speak; even the way he walked was quiet. That's what probably made him a great assassin for the Wharf Man in his previous job.

The group that they were following approached a large stone slab that was in the middle of a doorway. Julian stared at it and then turned back to face the small group of his underlings. "Seems important, doesn't it? Let's get it out of the way. See what's happening on the other side of that door."

A couple of the operatives got to work and pushed the slab of rock out of the way of the doorway. When it was pushed aside enough to see through, Julian put his face right up to the small opening and looked inside. Galen couldn't see what was on the other side, just darkness. Soon enough, they would have illuminated, but for now, they just had their own eyes to rely on; Julian's cold eyes stared hard into the darkness, trying to make out any shapes or images.

A wicked smile stretched across Julian's face, the kind of smile he only gave when he had some disturbing thought cross his mind. "I see it."

All of the operatives looked at one another, staring at Julian, who was the only one with any sort of view of what was behind the rock. They all waited with baited breath to hear what he had to say but he didn't seem to care about sharing with them.

"See what?" Galen finally asked with a roll of his eyes.

Julian turned back, that wicked grin still pasted on his visage.

"I see the altar."

Galen hoped that Julian was wrong. He didn't

want that arrogant bastard of a leader to get what he wanted. He didn't want him to be the one to kill Purdue and he definitely didn't want him to get to fulfill whatever his big wish was.

If Galen had his way, things would end very differently.

10

CHAPTER TEN – REUNIONS ON CRACKED ICE

Purdue hated whenever they had to go someplace cold. It was always difficult to go to a remote and desolate location but that was amplified whenever they were met by extreme weather conditions. They didn't just have to worry about where they were going or to watch where they were stepping. Now they had to worry about trying not to freeze to death. Succumbing to hypothermia was definitely not the most pleasant way to go.

Sam shivered beside him, adjusting his hat and the fur-lined hood pulled over it. In a place this far north, it really didn't matter how many layers they were wearing. No matter what they did, they were going to be cold.

The Moving Temple of Ah Puch loomed ahead of them, painted against the gray sky. Its dark stone walls stuck out against its white surroundings just as much as it had on the satellite images. It was just as Purdue remembered, but it looked so different in such a vastly different environment.

"How the hell is that even possible?" It just started to dawn on Sam how odd the temple's location was. It was one thing to see it on a screen or talk about it but to see it in person was something else entirely. That Mayan temple really didn't belong. But really, Sam should have spent less time thinking about his girlfriend back home and more thought on the temple that they were about to get to. "You're telling me that place bounces all over the world?"

"Aye...at least, that is what the old legends say. We've done this enough to know that most legends are at least partially true, haven't we?"

"Yes," Sam said. "That's very, very true. There's no one here."

Purdue had noticed that already and that had made his shivering body even tenser. It was strange considering all of the media attention that the temple had been getting. He was expecting to have to get by all kinds of reporters, camera operators, and police. Instead, there was nothing. On the one hand, he was glad to not have to deal with those kinds of obstacles, but on the other hand, it seemed very peculiar.

It was just them and the Mayan temple...and most likely the Order of the Black Sun as well. They were the only ones who had the resources and reach to get rid of all of the other potential onlookers. It was probably a trap. Only traps were this quiet.

Sure enough, there was a crunch behind them. Both Purdue and Sam turned around to find a dozen men clad in all white camouflage rising from the snowy ground. They'd been laying there in wait, ready for them to show up.

"Must have been really cold just hanging around out here," Purdue said casually, like he wasn't concerned at all by the newcomers. "Thankfully, it looks like you all dressed nice and warm."

The men didn't respond to his taunts. They all pointed their weapons at the two of them. The leader barked orders. "That's far enough, Purdue! Hands up! On your knees!"

The voice of the leader sounded familiar, but it was scratchy and hoarse.

"I said on your knees!" Despite the barking, the leader sounded a little unsure of his own authority, perhaps even somewhat afraid. "Now, Purdue! Now!"

"I'm not going to do that," Purdue said calmly. "But something's really bothering me...have we met before? I've got this weird feeling that we have."

The leader ripped off his mask and hood. The face wasn't immediately recognizable but Purdue knew he had seen it before. He knew he had spoken to this bald man before. Suddenly, it occurred to him. Being ambushed by this man was all too familiar. It's just that the last time, they were in a much warmer climate.

"Aw, yes, now I remember! Haven't we done this before? You were that Black Sun guy from Honduras. The one with the redhead." The mention of her sent a ripple of anger through the bald man. He sneered at Purdue, his eyes were wide with mania. He looked far less composed than Purdue remembered. "Yeah, that's you. That's definitely you. What was your name again? Lionel? Lucas? Lyle? It was definitely an 'L', aye? Or maybe not. I hate to tell you but you really didn't leave much of an impression at all. I should have recognized you right away...but instead...well...not so much."

"Lucius!" the man shrieked, gasping for breath like a rabid animal. "My name is Lucius! Where is Charlotte!? What did you do with her!?"

"Aw the lovely red haired girl from outside of the temple, aye? Yes, she was lovely and obviously smarter than you lot. I convinced her that it might be in her best interest not to stick around the Black Sun after a colossal failure like the one you pulled. She agreed. By now, she's probably on a nice beach somewhere, far away from this whole cult that Julian Corvus has turned the Order of the Black Sun into. Really, you should have done the same thing. You could probably use a nice vacation. You're not looking so well."

"Shut up! She wouldn't have left! She wouldn't!

She wouldn't! She wouldn't! She wouldn't! You're a liar, Purdue! A liar!"

He remembered Lucius as a calm and collected kind of guy, but he really only had known him for a few minutes, and much of that time was spent trying to prevent Lucius from killing him in the dark. They had gotten to know each other very well. But he certainly would have remembered if he was acting this wildly. He seemed off-balance and more than a little crazed. Even the other sentries around him seemed concerned.

Then again, the answer for his clear distress might be not far away. Purdue pointed at the Mayan temple. "You were there when it transported here. That must have been something, aye? Tell me, what did that feel like? Did it feel like flying real fast or was it just..." Purdue snapped his fingers. "Was it just like that? Instantly in the Arctic."

"More of the second..." Lucius seethed. "We were chasing you out the door when it moved. One second I was looking at you and Charlotte...green trees behind you...the next moment, all I could see was white...white everywhere. It was so cold. So, so cold. There was nothing. Nothing out here at all."

"Besides a musty old temple, aye? Must have been hard."

"Enough! Where is Charlotte!?"

"I told you," Purdue said with a sigh. "She's long gone. Took the high road and is probably better off for it."

"Purdue..." Sam muttered beside him, wanting

to get this over with. He didn't know Lucius or the situation so obviously wasn't nearly as interested by this conversation as Purdue was.

Purdue didn't exactly agree. He wanted some answers, especially from a man who had spent so long in that temple. "How did you survive out here on your own? There were others with you inside the temple when it transported away. Are these gentlemen them?"

"No," Lucius said firmly. "No, they are not."

"And they didn't survive the jump from Honduras to here like you did?"

"They made it here..." That loud mania grew much quieter and Lucius seemed like he wasn't really there anymore. He was back to a time that only existed in his memory, that the rest of the world didn't see. "But someone had to survive somehow. There was no food. None. No, no food. Someone had to survive. I made sure it was me."

"You killed them. Your own team." Purdue didn't doubt it.

From what parts of the other guards' faces they could see, it was clear that they were rather troubled by the news. They were waiting on orders from Lucius to open fire but they must have been doubting that those orders would ever come. They were at the mercy of his craziness.

One suddenly yelled, raising his weapon. "Enough talk! Let's waste them!"

"NO!" Lucius hissed. "No, not until he tells me where to find Charlotte."

"That again? Really?" Purdue was almost finding Lucius comical now. His insanity might have actually been funny if his unpredictability didn't make him so dangerous. "I think we best be moving along, aye? I know you probably came out here to settle that score, but get in line. There are plenty of people in the Order of the Black Sun that want my head. And admittedly, I've done far worse to them than I ever did to you."

"Shut up!"

As much as Purdue wanted to learn more about the Mayan temple, he was realizing that he wasn't going to learn anything of real value from Lucius. He may have spent a lot of time stuck in there, but it was most likely in the dark, where he did nothing but slowly slip into lunacy. If Purdue really wanted to learn more about the temple, then he would have to do it firsthand, with his own eyes. He could believe those much more than he could believe anything this deranged man said to him.

"You're not going to be seeing Charlotte again, sorry to say. We both know she'll be better for it. If it means anything, I really didn't mean for you to get trapped in this place. How was I supposed to know that the temple could hopscotch across the planet? And how was I supposed to know that it was going to happen while you were inside?"

Lucius' whole body was quaking, like it was at war with itself. His thoughts were probably bouncing off of the inside of his skull in confusion. All of that trauma, everything that happened to him had formed a twister inside of him. There would be no reasoning with him and this conversation was already hostile, and it was only going to get more so.

It was time to end it.

"I'm sorry for what happened. You shouldn't have been mixed up in all of this."

Unknown to the ambushers, Purdue had the pearl grasped tightly in his palm and the terrain they were walking on was just cold water—making it susceptible to the pearl's power. Purdue tightened his grip on the pearl and thought about the ice cracking under the armed guards. With that one thought, the ice gave way beneath them and they all dropped into the cold water. They never had a chance to even fire their weapons.

Lucius slipped into the water, splashing about but Purdue used the pearl's power to instantly freeze the water back into place. The Black Sun operatives were trapped under a sheer sheet of ice. There was no escaping for them. Purdue was Lucius' face pressed against the ice, screaming, drowning in the water. He was thrashing his hands against it but it wasn't going to shatter. Purdue felt a tinge of guilt as it wasn't a great way to go but they were all threatening their lives, and had harmed so many others. Still, he finally had to look away.

It was just Purdue and Sam again, alone in the frozen wastes.

"I'm glad you brought that along," Sam said

with a long sigh of relief. “That could have been messy without it.”

“Well, we weren't just going to storm the temple unarmed, aye? Suicide missions aren't something that I have any interest in partaking in. Far too wasteful, wouldn't you agree?”

Purdue could feel Mona Greer's book of shadows on him. It was so tempting to pull it out of his bag and just try to solve all of their problems with its dark magics. But for now, there was no need. The pearl's sway over water was enough to help them get by.

They continued trudging through the ice and snow toward the waiting temple ahead. Those guards could just be the first line of defense. The Order of the Black Sun was inside with potentially their entire forces with them. They may even have other ancient artifacts that could overpower the ones that Purdue carried. There was only one way to find out. They would have to get into the temple and see for themselves.

A silhouette was standing ahead of them, standing out against the white terrain. Purdue and Sam approached cautiously, their footsteps crunching in the snow, but braced themselves for whatever threat this would be. Purdue held the pearl firmly in his hand again, knowing it would be just as effective on this newcomer as it was against the group of scouts.

They drew closer and closer to the figure but when they reached it, they found a hooded silhouette facing the other direction and standing perfectly still. The sentry hadn't noticed their approach. That was a relief.

Purdue crept up on the guard and swung for a hard knock on the back of the head. The guard crumbled into a head in the snow far more easily than expected. In fact, the way the body fell didn't even seem human. When Purdue examined the person on the ground, he found nothing but a long parka and a pole.

It was nothing but a decoy—but for what?

Suddenly, someone tackled Purdue from behind.

"Purdue!" Sam shouted as Purdue and his attacker rolled through the snow together. He kicked the assailant off of him and his attacker got to his feet, facing him and Sam.

It was a face that Purdue recognized—the slim and slender figure of Oniel the once top enforcer of the crime boss, the Wharf Man. Purdue made the mistake of working with that crime ring during his most desperate time. When he fought back against the Wharf Man for trying to back stab him, he made an enemy of him and all of his followers. The ensuing fights ended with Purdue killing both the Wharf Man and Oniel's brother, Alton. Based on the glower that Oniel was staring at him with, he wasn't quite over either of their deaths.

Just like with Lucius, they had come across someone who had an ax to grind and who wanted

Purdue dead for past acts. But Oniel was far more dangerous than Lucius ever was.

Oniel was shivering, due to having used his parka for the decoy. All he had was a turtleneck shirt to keep him warm. He glared at Purdue with that same silent hatred that he always emanated with. His silence was due to his tongue being ripped out years ago. He had only ever spoken verbally to Purdue once and only to tell him that he would kill him, in a very broken, hard to understand series of sounds.

"Oniel..."

Oniel immediately drew a small dagger from his sleeve. He wasn't the chatty type, and he probably wouldn't be even if he had a tongue. His brother used to do all of the talking for him, but Purdue had silenced him forever.

"It's been awhile," Purdue said, clutching the pearl tightly in his hand. "Last time I saw you, you were treading water. I should have made sure you drowned, just like I did your boss. I was hoping you would smarten up and leave me alone after I got rid of the Wharf Man. Obviously, you didn't smarten up."

Oniel took a murderous step forward but then stopped again, like he was waiting for the perfect chance to pounce.

"You saw what I did to those other scouts, right? That's why you set up that coat trap...but did you see how I beat your friends?" Purdue opened his hand and displayed the pearl. "You remember this, don't you? What it did to the Wharf Man's submarine? What it did to him? You can't win this fight, Oniel. Walk away."

Oniel took another step forward, clearly not convinced by Purdue's argument.

"Fine then. Your choice, aye? I know you're not a conversationalist but I'm glad we have a chance to talk. Imagine my surprise when I found out the Order of the Black Sun knew I was alive...and then imagine my surprise when Julian tells me that you were the one who told them about my survival. You were pissed, I get that. But did you really have to go running to them?"

"Who is this guy?" Sam asked nervously beside him.

"Someone I met during my time when I was homeless. He ran with some really bad bastards...who I have since gotten rid of. I imagine that he's holding something of a grudge against me. Isn't that right, Oniel? You want me dead?"

Oniel gave a firm single nod of his head.

"The knife already made that kind of obvious, don't you think?" Sam said cautiously. "You have a terrible habit of making enemies, you know that?"

"It's one of my many gifts," Purdue said.

Oniel stared at them, his beady eyes flickering from one to the other, like he was deciding who he was going to disembowel first. Purdue would imagine that he would want to kill him first, since he wanted his vengeance for his brother but he also knew that Oniel was violent enough to completely mutilate a stranger like Sam just for sport. He and his late brother were feared for just how brutal they were to anyone that they were targeting. They were the perfect instruments of death for a dangerous criminal like the Wharf Man. Now, without his original crew to help him channel his affinity for violence, Oniel seemed to have given his talents over to the Order of the Black Sun instead.

"You're not going to win this fight," Purdue said, again showing the pearl. "There is frozen water all around it. One thought from me, and I could have you drowning just like the Wharf Man. Walk away, Oniel. I know you have your grudge but my fight with the Black Sun doesn't involve you. I'll even forgive you telling them that I was alive...and that caused a whole lot of problems for me."

Oniel took two steps forward this time, rejecting his offer to leave.

"Aye," Purdue said, cupping the pearl in his palm. "Let's get this over with then. I have better vendettas to deal with than yours."

Oniel charged at the two of them but Purdue was ready. He thought about ice rising up to shield them and just as he did, the pearl's power pulled a sheet of ice in front of them, intercepting Oniel's blade.

"Thank god for that pearl!" Sam shouted, taking a few steps backward. He didn't have any sort of weapon to fight Oniel off with, especially not a magical pearl that could control water.

Purdue lowered the wall of ice and Oniel tried

another strike but Purdue had a surge of water spray up from the ice and knock the knife out of Oniel's grasp.

"I know you said you would kill me..." Purdue said calmly. "But that's not going to be today. Why not leave and try again another time. Right now, I've got bigger concerns. And to be honest, I think your anger is misplaced. Your boss and your brother were both terrible people that hurt far more people than they helped. The world is a better place with them gone." It was cold but he had very little desire to be gentle with an assassin hell-bent on murdering him.

Oniel pulled another knife from his other sleeve.

"You're a persistent bastard, aye?" Purdue rubbed his face in annoyance.

Purdue caused more water to burst out from under them and manipulated it to pour over Oniel like a hose. The force of the water knocked Oniel off his feet and sliding across the ice. He rolled on the ground, soaked from head to toe by the water. He got back up but was shivering more violently now. If he didn't get somewhere warm quick, he would probably die from hypothermia.

"Enough of this."

Oniel, silent as ever, didn't seem to mind that his body was freezing. All he cared about was his vengeance, and making it as painful as possible for Purdue. He was focused on the one objective and he wasn't going to stop until the deed was done or he was physically incapable continuing. If he kept this up, he would die out here in the cold.

"I'll give you one last chance. Stop this now."

Oniel shook his head and opened his mouth. He spoke with the same hoarse sounds that he had the last time he delivered a message to Purdue—and it was the same message.

"K-kii—ouu."

Kill you—Purdue wasn't going to let that happen.

"No. You're not."

An eruption of water spurted out from the ice and rose into the air, high above Oniel, forming an enormous wave. With another thought, Purdue brought that wave down on Oniel. The assassin was caught in its force, being dragged across the ice back toward the temple.

"Damn," Sam whistled. "That was impressive. Is he dead?"

"I'm not sure," Purdue said honestly. "But I'm sure we'll find out. Shall we?"

They continued their trek toward the temple, knowing that Oniel was nothing more than part of a first line of defense. The things that they would find inside would probably be much more dangerous than him. Now that he was with the Order of the Black Sun, Oniel wasn't nearly as scary. It didn't help that his boss was an immortal psychopath who now controlled one of the most dangerous collections of people on the planet. Oniel went from being a top enforcer in a crime ring to nothing more than another cog in a much, much larger machine.

Purdue hoped to walk by Oniel's shivering, unconscious body in the snow, still soaked from the wave he had thrown at him but there was no sign of him. He had probably retreated back into the temple. Perfect—another enemy to still have to worry about. He should just trapped him under the ice like he had done to the other guards outside. Now, Oniel could warn the others inside about their arrival but Oniel definitely wasn't going to be able to shout his warnings to the whole place, so his warnings might be somewhat delayed.

Purdue wished that the wave would cause a bit more significant and lasting damage than it apparently had. He wouldn't have shed a single tear if that surge of water had killed Oniel either. The man had spent his whole life cutting people down, and had since joined a group that had killed plenty more. It would have probably been a service to everyone else if Oniel was taken out for good. All he seemed to contribute to the planet was murder.

It said a lot that such a dangerous man was a small part of Julian Corvus' order. He'd made the Black Sun a far more dangerous group, and they were heading straight into what would probably be a swarm of them.

11

CHAPTER ELEVEN – THE PERFORMANCE

Purdue and Sam approached the entrance to the temple. It was surprising that they didn't come across any more of the Black Sun guards. Maybe they thought Lucius and his group would be a sturdy enough defense. They may have been if not for Lucius' less than stellar leadership. His mania had taken priority over his mission and cost him. Now he and his men were popsicles in the frigid waters below. It was Julian's own fault for trusting a man who so clearly wasn't right in the head. It wasn't a good idea to give a man who just spent weeks isolated, freezing, and starving to death a weapon and trust him to perform well. There had to be someone better to patrol the temple's perimeter. Hell, all of the men he was barking orders at were probably more suited for the job at hand.

Maybe that's what Oniel was supposed to be but he was a sadist who only cared about slitting

Purdue's throat rather than actually protecting the temple. He wouldn't have been an ideal choice either for ensuring that no intruders came to disturb their plans.

It was odd that the Order of the Black Sun's outer defenses were so minimal. Then again, it might have just felt that way. For all they really knew, dozens of guards were lying in wait, hidden in the snow. They could just be watching for the right moment to pounce or spring a trap. Or allowing Purdue and Sam to enter the temple might have been the trap.

They were bound to find out soon enough. Purdue expected Julian Corvus and all of his cronies to be waiting for them the second that he and Sam walked inside but was relieved that he couldn't see anyone at all nearby.

The interior of the Mayan temple looked quite a bit different than Purdue remembered from his brief time inside during his trek to Honduras. For one thing, he could actually see this time. The Order of the Black Sun had lit up the whole place like a Christmas tree. Purdue had only been inside for a few minutes last time and he had spent those few moments in nearly complete darkness. The Black Sun wanted to see what they were doing and what exactly this place really had to offer them.

Purdue wondered if they had found the sacrificial altar yet. If they had, why hadn't Julian's wish been made? Or maybe they didn't even know that part of the story...but that didn't seem very likely. Purdue had found that bit of information with ease so it shouldn't have been difficult for them. They had teams of researchers devoted to learning anything could about relics that could be useful to their cause. They must have known about the temple's real importance. How could they not?

"Nice place," Sam muttered beside him but looked more than a little disgusted by their new surroundings. "Very cozy. Think Nina is somewhere in here?"

"I doubt it," Purdue said, keeping his voice down just in case anyone was nearby. He wearily kept looking up and down the narrow corridors. The Black Sun did a fine job lighting the place up but there were still plenty of lingering shadows that an enemy could creep out of. "They would probably have her, Charles, and Jean-Luc Gerard locked up some place secure, like wherever their headquarters is. I don't think even Julian is moronic enough to bring them here. It's not secure at all..."

"But they would be perfect bait."

"True," Purdue said, knowing full well that Julian might try to spring some sick trap like that on them. It was definitely his style, but it also would be a gamble. "That is if they're still alive..."

Sam frowned. "They have to be..."

Purdue wanted to believe that too. Sometimes he had to. Otherwise so much of his efforts would have been for nothing. If their friends were dead, then it didn't matter if they beat Julian Corvus and the Order of the Black Sun—they would already have lost.

A sound burst down the corridor. It sounded like something had dropped and hit the floor hard. Purdue stared down the hall in the direction that the noise had come from. Purdue pictured an entire legion of enemies waiting around the corner, and imagined that one of them had dropped their gun. They were probably all shushing one another and trying their best to stay hidden.

Purdue and Sam waited a long moment, hoping that someone would show themselves but no one did. Whatever that noise had come from, they weren't going to get any answers easily. They cautiously walked down the hall in the direction that the sound originated from. Purdue pulled the book of shadows out of his bag and flipped it open. He held his free hand out in front of him, ready to cast one of the many spells from inside that witch's private journal. He wasn't very experienced with the black magics inside but any magic to use as a weapon was better than being completely weaponless against a possible and probable ambush.

They turned the corner and the both of them braced themselves to be staring down a whole platoon of Black Sun troops but there was no one there after all. They both let out a sigh of relief and continued down the next corridor. Based on the light fixtures that had been placed in this corridor, the Black Sun had clearly already been through there. For all they knew, the Black Sun members were on the complete opposite end of the temple, too busy setting up lights to put up much of a defense. That was good. If they could just get to the altar first, then Purdue could use the book of shadows to quickly incapacitate one of the Black Sun goons. With magic, he had no doubt he could kill at least one of them on the altar with ease. And if the stories were true, that was all they needed to do to activate their chance at a wish.

The pair of them came to a doorway that had a large rock beside it. That slab of stone acted as something of a door but had been pushed aside, allowing access to whatever was on the other side. Purdue and Sam entered an enormous chamber, but only after poking their heads inside first and making sure that the coast was clear. A huge room like that made it easy for someone to spot them, or for someone to hide. Either way, an ambush would really put a great big wrench into their plans.

When everything seemed okay, the two proceeded into the room. It was different than the tight corridors they had been moving through and Purdue got the distinct impression that the entire temple had been constructed around this particular chamber. It just seemed so open, like it was meant to house a large number of people—like a football stadium being made to house thousands of fans. They entered through one of the four doorways that were on each side of the chamber. They came through the west-most doorway; the other doorways made him nervous. Someone could easily be on the other side of those openings, waiting to pour in.

There was nothing in the stone room besides a large stone slab in the very center of it. That must have been the altar, the one he'd read so much about. If they could perform a sacrifice at that altar, then the Moving Temple of Ah Puch's power would grant them one wish. It had been hard to imagine before, but now, staring at the slab of rock planted in the floor, it still didn't feel real. They were so close to being able to repair all of the damage that had been done to their lives.

The slab of stone that made up the altar had cracks in it that seemed precise—perhaps even man-made—and looked to be where the blood spilled from the sacrifice would seep into the altar and activate the temple's powers.

Suddenly, the room echoed with muffled cries, and when they turned around, Sam's face grew very pale, his whole body tensed up, and his mind was struggling to process the reality of what he was seeing.

Purdue could tell just from Sam's expression what was going on.

Kendra was there—and there was a knife at her throat.

THAT WASN'T RIGHT. She couldn't have been there.

She was back home waiting for him, just like she said she would be. She had to be...but the Black Sun operative with an arm around her and holding a blade at her neck said otherwise. The Order of the Black Sun had found her, found an easy weapon to use against Sam. How? He had been so careful to still keep mostly hidden even when he was with Kendra. It was far from a public relationship. Hell, they had spent most of their glorious time together in bed. Those rooms he stayed in had become slices of paradise when Kendra was around. This was different. Kendra's presence in this situation felt much more like some sort of hell.

He was so used to that beautiful woman smiling at him but he couldn't see her smile now. Her mouth was taped over, hiding those lips he had kissed so many times. All he could focus on were her eyes, which were brimming with wet tears.

"Welcome, Purdue. Cleave," the Black Sun operative said with a Cheshire grin. "We were hoping you would show up at some point. I imagine you got here without any issues. No problems on the road?" He said it with a knowing wink, well aware that they had probably come across Lucius and the sentries outside in the snow.

"No problems at all," Purdue said. "A few minor inconveniences, aye...but nothing serious."

"How about now, Cleave?" The man said, bringing his attention to Sam and laughing when he spoke. He pressed the knife closer to Kendra's skin. "Have you run into any problems today?"

Sam wanted to tear that man's throat out and shut him up for good. He couldn't believe that they had found her. It shouldn't have been possible yet there she was. They'd dragged his new lady friend all the way up to the Arctic for no other reason than to use as a weapon against him. Why? They already had Nina, Charles, and that occult expert that Purdue had mentioned a few times. They had plenty of other potential hostages that they could have brought along instead...but they had to take her too. That was just like the Julian Corvus he remembered from Rhodes—unrelenting and not having any depths that he wouldn't stoop to in order to get what he wanted.

It did make him worry a little though. Maybe it wasn't a matter of how many hostages they had and instead they had actually needed one since Nina and the others were dead. He didn't want to believe it, but at this point, he wouldn't have been shocked if they were already far too late to save their friends. But they still had to try, and now they had to save Kendra too.

"Don't touch her," Sam growled. "You let her go. Now."

"Why would I do that?" The man snickered, moving the blade even closer to her flesh. "She's right where she needs to be, don't you think?"

"Pardon me," Purdue interrupted. "I don't believe we've met, have we? All of you Black Sun lads look the same to me. It's hard to keep track of who is who. I only remember Corvus because he wears nicer suits than the rest of you. But no, I really don't think we've met. I'd remember an ugly mug like yours, my friend."

"I'm Boris," the man said, licking his lips like a hungry animal. "And you two are well known to me. I've spent a lot of time learning all about you. Anything I could find out to make be of better service to Julian."

"Ah," Purdue snickered. "You're one of Julian's puppets. God, we keep bumping into so many of you. You want my advice, you need to cut those strings and start thinking for yourselves. Does wonders for you."

Purdue looked down at the page that was open in the book of shadows. He didn't want to risk turning the page or Boris might cut that girl's throat so he had to make do with what his eyes could already see when he looked down. There was one spell that might be able to do the trick. It would pop this Boris guy like a balloon. Sure, his insides would explode all over Sam's girlfriend, but he definitely wouldn't be able to hold that knife to her throat anymore.

"I wouldn't recommend it," Boris said threateningly. "Correct me if I'm wrong, but you're no warlock, are you? No regular Harry Potter. And from what I know from that kind of magic...it's a tricky thing to control. And one mistake and you could kill yourself or everyone in the room. So if you're thinking of using one of those incantations on me...just remember...you might just hurt this girl too...and you don't want that, do you sweetheart?"

Boris ripped the duct tape off of Kendra's lips and she let out a yelp of pain. Her sobs and heavy breaths were far louder now as she gasped for air. She looked at Sam desperately but then she looked down at the blade hovering under her chin.

"Please..." she said.

Sam's heart almost broke right then. He had never seen her like that and he had hoped never to see her like that. She had nothing to do with any of it. She shouldn't have been there.

"I could just surprise you," Purdue said nonchalantly, still looking down at the open page in front of him. He did his best to try and memorize the strange words that he was seeing. The gruesome and crude drawing beside it showed what would happen well enough. That witch Mona Greer was certainly a very talented artist. "For all you know, I've spent my time in hiding rereading the Harry Potter novels every day. I may just be a full-fledged sorcerer now, aye? Maybe I'll turn you into a goddamn frog. How does that sound?"

"No, you won't," Boris laughed, craning his head behind Kendra's using her as a human shield. "You wouldn't risk it."

"It's never a smart move to doubt me," Purdue said, smirking. "I make poor decisions quite often."

Purdue raised his free hand threateningly and started muttering the incantation from off the page.

Boris' eyes widened with newfound terror and he hid himself even more behind the crying woman. Purdue tried to focus but he was admittedly nervous about how this was going to go. He hoped that he could make this work, but it was almost just as likely that Sam's new girlfriend would explode too. But he wouldn't let this bastard do this.

Sam stared at Purdue, surprised that he was going through with it. Despite his claims, Purdue was definitely not a sorcerer, he wasn't even an amateur street magician. He had no real experience harnessing any sort of magic at all. And Purdue had told him multiple times how dangerous that book of shadows was. It was a threat to everyone around it, not just the one reading from it. One wrong word and Purdue could kill everyone in the room.

Kendra was weeping, staring at Purdue with fear. She thought she was going to die. If not by the knife at her neck than by the magic that was about to be thrown at her. She was sobbing uncontrollably. It was a stressful situation in general but for her...she was probably so confused. Sam felt so bad that he had let it come to this, that his enemies had become hers.

Her quiet cries turned into scared screams.

"Stop!" Sam yelled over her heartbreaking shrieks. "Don't do it, Purdue!"

Purdue glanced at him. "Calm down, aye? I've got this."

"No you don't! Put the book down!" Sam barked. "Now!"

"Yeah, put it down, Purdue!" Boris cackled. "Listen to your friend!"

Purdue looked at him but then back to the book and kept chanting. He wasn't giving Sam much of a choice—no—that bastard wasn't giving him any choice at all. Sam swiped hard with both his hands at the book and knocked Mona Greer's spell book flying out of Purdue's hands and across the room.

"Oi!" He snapped at Sam but Sam just shook his head.

"Are you crazy? You're not going to risk that! You're not!"

Purdue looked over at the book of shadows like he was contemplating going to go pick it up but then backed down. He looked a little embarrassed and also pissed but Sam wouldn't let Purdue run this situation. It wasn't his girlfriend in danger. He didn't get to put her life in danger or make the decision that might get her killed.

"Sorry..." Purdue mumbled, clenching his fists.

Sam understood that Purdue wanted to get rid of the Black Sun and this might have been their chance to go through with his plan. Purdue no doubt wanted to use the magic to incapacitate Boris and then kill him on the altar to get their wish, and that may have been a good plan...if Kendra wasn't there. That changed everything. They were far more vulnerable than they had been when they first entered the temple.

Sam couldn't stand seeing Kendra look so afraid. Tears rolled down her cheeks and her mouth was trembling as she tried to keep her composure from completely falling apart. She shouldn't have been there. She had nothing to do with any of it. He could only imagine how confused and scared she must have been.

"Don't hurt her!" Sam roared.

"Sam..." Purdue spoke softly beside him. He sounded incredibly calm given the hostage situation they were now facing. Purdue didn't look at him as he spoke; he just stared at Kendra. "You don't really believe this horseshit, do you?"

Sam thought he misheard at first but Purdue kept staring at Kendra. He didn't look nervous or scared. In fact, he looked scarily at ease with the whole situation. A small smile even curled on the corner of his lips.

"She's not that bad of an actress, I'll give her that."

"The hell are you talking about?" Sam asked through his clenched jaw. Kendra was at risk of being killed at any second and his friend was being so callous. This wasn't the time for Purdue's games. Sam tried to walk forward but Purdue put an arm in front of him, blocking his path.

Purdue finally looked at him, but only long enough to roll his eyes and then peered back at the panicked woman being held captive. "You really are not the most observant man, my friend."

Purdue started clapping his hands until he was a one-man audience giving incredibly enthusiastic applause. He was acting like he'd just attended the greatest performance of all time; a definite five-star award winning show.

"You see...we've met before. Your lady friend and I. She tried to work her charm on me..." Purdue spoke up, addressing the hostage directly. "In that book shop, remember? Right before you sent a Black Sun killer after me. You were a scout. You were probably hoping I wouldn't remember...but I don't forget a face, especially a deceivingly pretty one like yours."

Sam listened intently, hanging onto every word. He stopped trying to push through and let what he was hearing sink in. Purdue wouldn't be this adamant unless he was absolutely certain—so maybe he was. As much as Sam hated what Purdue was implying, he'd worked with him long enough to know that he should hear him out. He should at least see where he was going with all of this.

Kendra's tear-filled eyes look to Sam again, pleading for help. But when he didn't move and it was clear that he was going to hear Purdue out, the crying came to an abrupt halt. There were no more wails or pleas. The tears seemed to roll back up into her eye sockets. She let out a long sigh but then smirked, like a child being deciding to admit to a prank.

"Let go of me." The Black Sun operative holding her captive immediately released her upon her command. He took a step back and Kendra started giggling. "I have to hand it to you, Purdue. You have quite the memory."

"Thanks."

Sam's insides twisted. Purdue really was right; Kendra part of the Order of the Black Sun. All of that time they had spent together wasn't real. She had been faking the whole thing—using him. It had all been a lie; every single moment of it. He'd fallen for it like an idiot.

"Sorry, Sam," Purdue said and glanced at him with some pity. "She's quite stunning. I don't blame you for not being able to see past that. She played you like a fiddle my friend. Used you to keep tabs on us for Corvus."

"It wasn't hard," Kendra said with glee. "You were so desperate to feel loved, to feel needed. All of those insecurities of yours are all over you. So easy to play with."

"Go to hell.."

"Aw, did I really hurt you? It's your own fault."

"Just shut up."

There was clapping but it wasn't Purdue this time. Julian Corvus emerged from the shadows of the chamber. He had been watching it all unfold and looked to have been enjoying the show quite a bit. "She is very good, isn't she? A wonderful addition to the order."

Sam spat on the floor. "Scum attracts scum."

"Always so rude," Julian said and looked to both Sam and Purdue. "Mr. Purdue. Mr. Cleave. It's always a pleasure to bump into you. What brings you this far north?" He knew full well why there were there. "Ah, of course! This temple, yes? A marvel, to be sure...but that's not it, is it? No, you came looking for a fight, didn't you? You came looking to settle old scores. That's quite convenient. I have scores of my own that I would like to bring some closure to. You trapped me under those ruins the last time we saw each other, Mr. Purdue. If not for my...inability to die, I would have...well...how do I put this...been dead."

"Still doesn't come close to what you've done to me," Purdue growled. "Stealing my things. Burning down my home. Abducting my friends."

"The list goes on and on, I'm sure," Julian said with demented laugh that started to shatter his otherwise magnetic charisma. "We've both wounded the other, haven't we? My strikes just cut deeper than yours. So let's end this here. This temple will serve as a perfect arena for one last battle with you."

"Fine by me," Purdue said.

"We have to be smart about this," Sam mumbled beside him.

"Aye, and the smart thing to do would be to get rid of him forever."

Julian took in their surroundings. "Yes, it's perfect. You would be the perfect candidate for sacrifice. The key to unlocking this temple's real power and purpose. Your death will make my dreams a reality. It's poetic, isn't it?"

Purdue spat on the floor. "Do your worst, you bastard...but get over yourself. You're not a fucking poet."

12

CHAPTER TWELVE – THE ALTAR

It didn't take long for the Order of the Black Sun to lay Purdue down on top of the sacrificial altar, strapping him down flat on his back, waiting to be killed. The stone slab wasn't exactly comfortable, either.

Sam was tied to a pillar a few yards away. He was still struggling, trying to wrestle his way out of his bindings, constantly shifting his shoulders and arms about, but didn't seem to be making any actual progress toward an escape. He was no Houdini.

"I knew your girlfriend was too good to be true," Purdue laughed. "I knew it!"

"Oh shut up. You didn't know for sure."

"It was kind of obvious wasn't it? Who would be that interested in you, aye? No one, that's who."

Sam ignored him and didn't respond. He obviously didn't want to have this conversation right now. He was still probably processing that particularly nasty betrayal. It was just like Mama May had said about blades being in backs. There was definitely a knife in the back of Sam right now, and it was in deep.

"How do we let this happen?" Sam groaned through his gritted teeth. "We're better than this!"

"Are we?" Purdue asked casually, just staring up at the dark ceiling. Things were looking bleak and he was struggling to see a real way out of this mess. "If we were, you think we could have done something right. I brought a pearl that can control water—hell the whole ocean itself—and a book filled with magic spells that can literally turn people to ash if I wanted it to. Both of those artifacts are some of the most powerful things on the planet. This should have been easy...yet here we are...two incompetent assholes, aye?"

Sam stopped his struggling for a moment and managed a little chuckle. "We definitely are...but at least we've got each other."

"Hooray for us."

Purdue gently tapped the back of his head against the stone underneath where he lay. It was the only real movement he could manage. Part of him felt like throwing his head back so hard that he just cracked his skull open. That would get all of this over with and he wouldn't have to wait to be inevitably murdered by his enemies. Robbing Julian and the rest of the Black Sun of the chance of killing him was a fun thought. They would be so angry.

"Hey..." Purdue said, still tapping his head absent-mindedly. "Do you think if smash my skull on this altar, that it will count as a good enough blood sacrifice to get my wish?"

"I doubt it...I'm sure you have to actually die and it's not a matter of just blood. I suppose if you did that but made your wish just as you died, there might be a chance to get your wish. Or I could make the wish for you maybe."

"So I bash my own head open and you wish for us to escape and for me to be alive..." The plan sounded so ludicrous as it left Purdue's mouth.

The two of them started laughing and throwing out even more nonsensical ideas for escape.

"Maybe we can convince Julian to kill someone else to get his wish. After all, his life is going to be so boring without me."

"I think he's already pretty determined to make sure that you're the sacrifice," Sam said. "As for me...who the hell knows what's going to happen to me."

Someone was approaching. The sound of tapping drew closer as something repeatedly rapped against the stone floors of the temple.

Purdue couldn't crane his head enough to see who it was but he didn't have to. Within moments, Galen Fitzgerald was looming over him, craning his head so that he was right in his line of vision, looking down on him.

"You aren't looking too good, Davy."

Purdue hadn't missed the Irishman. He hadn't missed having to listen to an insecure narcissist complain about how Purdue had insulted him at every turn. The truth was, Purdue only ever thought of Galen as an egotistical prick. They were never business rivals. They were never friends. Galen tried so hard to prove that he was the best but never understood that his toxic ambition and need for validation were exactly why he never succeeded.

"If this really is it for you...for real this time...I wanted to be able to have one last chat between us old friends."

Purdue couldn't contain a loud snort. "We weren't friends, Galen. We never, ever were. We were acquaintances at best. And even that's just me being generous."

"Of course we weren't," Galen said from above him but was very visibly seething. "The great and powerful David Purdue is too good for friends. He's too busy looking at down at the rest of the world. You always thought I was so small compared to you."

"Yes. I did."

Galen looked dumbfounded by Purdue's bluntness but Purdue wasn't going to be polite about it. "Not because I'm some arrogant bastard, no. But because you are a slimy conniving little rat who is trying way too hard to be a peacock. It'll never happen. You're always trying to climb your way to the top even if it means completely selling out. I mean look at you. You joined forces with the people who permanently crippled your leg. They blew it to hell with bullets and you still kiss their asses. All so you can get a pat on the head and feel like you're even a little important."

"Shut your mouth, Davy."

"It's the truth. You're not better than me. You should at least realize that by now. Especially not when you're just Julian Corvus's lapdog. "

"I am not his lapdog! You think I don't know what he is? He's a proper loon, that one, and I'm only keeping him around for a wee bit longer. He wants you dead...and seems he's going to get that...but I want you dead even more than he does."

Purdue managed a grin, letting it shine big and bright to the man standing over him. "I'm flattered."

Galen ignored that smile. "And if he kills you on this altar, they say he'll get whatever he wants. His heart's desire. I imagine that bastard will wish for world domination. So he'll not only get to kill you, but also fulfill all of his dreams. That doesn't seem fair, does it? What about what I want?"

"You should realize by now that no one really gives a damn what you want, Galen."

Purdue had never been afraid of the Irishman. He mostly just found all of his grandstanding irritating. He was always a lot of bark without much bite; nothing more than a spoiled brat with a lot of big claims. But there was something new now —something actually dangerous.

Galen picked up the old sacrificial knife and looked it over in his fingers. "If I put this in you, I have the pleasure of killing you and then I'll get to wish for whatever I want. I wouldn't exactly have to worry about repercussions from Julian, eh? Not if I can just wish him out of existence."

It was a surprisingly bold strategy for someone as small minded as Galen Fitzgerald, and maybe he was desperate enough to try it.

"But if all of these legends about this place are nothing more than bullocks...then the order will kill you for killing me."

"Aye," Galen let out a quiet giggle. "But at least I'd still have killed you. I'm the most deserving one after all. Not Julian. You should be mine to kill."

That was obviously what was most important to Galen—and that made Purdue slightly nervous.

Galen still looked at the gleam of the blade in his hand. "I did promise Oniel that he could cut off some pieces of you too so I'd have to take that into consideration. You've made a lot of enemies, Davy."

"This is all inspirational but stop your teasing. If you're going to end me and all that...then get the hell on with it already!"

Galen's fingers tightened around the sacrificial blade and Purdue braced himself as best as he could. Seeing the contempt in Galen's eyes, Purdue had no doubt that the dagger would have come for him if not for a sudden shout.

"Mr. Fitzgerald!"

Julian Corvus stormed into the chamber with a number of other Black Sun lackeys flanking him.

"You are not supposed to be here."

Galen lowered the knife. "I couldn't miss a chance for a front row seat to Davy's execution, now could I?"

Julian held out his hand, expecting for the blade to be turned over to him. Galen hesitated, glancing down at the vulnerable Purdue on the altar. If he could just quickly stab Purdue and make his wish, he could take complete control of the whole situation. Maybe being called Julian's lapdog had gotten to him.

After a long moment of uncertainty, Galen handed the dagger to Julian and limped a few steps away. Julian's gray eyes stared at the Irishman as he stepped aside. Even he looked alarmed by how long it had taken to be given the blade. After Galen was a safe number of steps away, Julian averted his attention back to Purdue on the altar.

"Your death will come very soon, Mr. Purdue. We're just waiting for a few minor things to be put in place."

"And what about me?" Sam spoke up. "Since I don't get the honor of being a human sacrifice."

Kendra smiled at Sam from behind Julian, mixed in with the other Black Sun operatives at his side. It was a horrid smile, twisting across her otherwise beautiful face. "WE haven't decided yet. But we will."

"Sir!" A Black Sun operative sprinted into the chamber. "There is a chopper preparing to land outside!"

"Who is it?"

"We were given Elijah Dane's confirmation code."

13

CHAPTER THIRTEEN – THE CAVALRY COMES

The helicopter's blades whirled overhead and Nina listened to the thumping sounds they made. It was nice to have something to focus on besides her own nervousness. They had finally escaped...they should probably have been running as far away from the Order of the Black Sun as they could, and scatter to the farthest corners of the Earth. Instead, they were heading straight back to their captors. Maybe they were crazy, suffering from some form of Stockholm Syndrome where they couldn't just leave the people that kept them as prisoners for so long. Whatever the case, they were risking far more than she wanted to be risking, but they didn't have a choice.

Elijah had filled her and the others in on the real power of the Mayan temple that the Black Sun was investigating. If a sacrifice was performed inside of that temple, then a wish could be granted

—supposedly any wish. Nina didn't know how that worked, but she wasn't shocked to see something unexplained be real. That was what she had seen all the time since she started exploring the world with Purdue and Sam.

There was one bit about the temple though, that Elijah claimed that Julian and the rest of the Order of the Black Sun were not even privy to. At least as far as he knew. There was something that they hadn't taken into account that he only knew thanks to one of the old texts inside the deep vault. There wasn't much information about the Moving Temple of Ah Puch in the world but this piece of text pointed to a scenario that could really put a wrench into Julian's plans. But if Julian became aware of it, then they were looking at a doomsday scenario again.

Julian Corvus and the Order of the Black Sun had to be stopped now. If they weren't, then the whole world could be at risk. Julian could possibly use this Mayan temple's power to shape reality to his will—to get whatever he wanted. Nina knew him well enough to know that Julian wasn't the kind of man who wanted anything good.

Charles didn't seem to share her train of thought. The older man groaned behind her. "Can anyone please tell me why we are going anywhere near those horrible people again?"

Nina perked up. "Because we might be the only ones who can stop those horrible people from making the rest of the world just as horrible."

"Precisely," Elijah said beside her, with that same condescending tone that he usually spoke down to people with. "Believe me, you don't want Julian to go through with the plans he has in mind. They're far from ideal for anyone who isn't him."

Charles was usually so respectful, patient, and mild-mannered but his time at the bottom of a hole in the Black Sun base had chipped some of that away. There was a harshness and an impatience to him now. Or maybe he just wanted to be able to take a nice shower after months of being deprived.

"Begging your pardons, but why bring me along?"

"We didn't exactly have time to drop you off," Jean said calmly.

"I just have no desire to have to see any of those mongrels' wretched faces ever again...they shot me in the head, brought me back to the land of the living with the spear that pierced Jesus Christ himself, giving me immortality, and then tossed me into a hole and left me there. I couldn't even die down there."

"I know, Charles. I know..." Nina tried to speak with some tact. "What they've done to all of us is awful. That's why we can't let them continue."

Jean put a hand on Charles's shoulder. "If it makes you feel better...you can't exactly be killed anymore. So you have that going for you. You'll have nothing to worry about if this turns into a big fight, my friend. Nothing at all."

"Besides..." Nina started, not really sure what

was going to come out of her mouth but she hoped it would be convincing enough to get him to stop his complaining. "If Purdue is there, don't you want to help him?"

Charles nearly flinched at the thought. All of those worries he had seemed to slip right off his wrinkly face, replaced by a remembrance of a time when he was just a butler, doing his best to help his boss.

"Of course I want to help him..."

"Then stop your whining," Nina said bluntly. You won't just be helping Purdue. You'll be helping everyone. And don't you want to bring down the Order of the Black Sun?"

The old man scratched his chin. "If we are being honest, I would much rather be home with a nice book in my hands. Something pleasant to read."

"They burned down your home, Chuck," Jean said with an awkward laugh. "So they took away that possibility too."

Charles relented and gave a grave, worried nod of his head. "Fine, fine. Let's get on with it quickly then."

"You really didn't have a choice in the matter," Elijah said coldly. "I'm the one flying the helicopter."

Nina smiled and everyone else in the chopper followed suit. At least they were all on the same page. Jean was right about Charles too. Despite his advanced age, his newfound immortality could be very useful, especially when Julian Corvus had the his own eternal durability that they would have to worry about.

Now that the debate was settled, Nina let the hum of the spinning blades above lure her back to sleep, knowing that it could be the last time she got any rest.

NINA WOKE up to Jean tapping her. “Wake up. We're here.”

When the haze of her drowsiness wore off and lifted, Nina looked out of the window at an enormous dark structure settled in the midst of an icy landscape. It looked so wrong, like seeing a skyscraper in the middle of a grassy field.

“So what's the plan then?”

“I go in first,” Elijah said solemnly. “Make some sort of distraction. I'll come up with some reason that I decided to come. While I do that, you all sneak around as best as you can.”

It wasn't a great plan, but it was better than fighting their way in head on. At least this way, they weren't going to be immediately gunned down.

When the helicopter landed, Nina could feel herself tensing up. This was it. The fight that she had anticipated for so long. Every day she spent wasting away in that dungeon, she had imagined what it would be like to be free and to fight the people that had turned her into their prisoner. For one thing, she imagined a warmer climate but this would have to do. By the end of the day, she wanted to have Julian Corvus locked in a cell and to be looking at him from the other side of the bars. He may not have been able to die...so if she couldn't kill him, putting him through what he did to her would be a good enough revenge.

"Everyone ready?"

"No," Charles said bluntly. "I wish I was at home with a nice drink and my favorite book in my hands."

"I know," Elijah said coldly. "But beggars can't be choosers. We all hate the Order of the Black Sun. We all hate Julian. Let's show them just how much we hate them."

Nina smiled. "Gladly."

THE PLAN STARTED off well enough. Elijah got out of the helicopter and met a few Black Sun operatives in the snow, halfway between the chopper and the temple. While he was speaking with them, hopefully making up some convincing scenario that would explain his arrival, the others began their attempts to get into the temple undetected. Nina led the way as the three of them kept low and used the multiple helicopters surrounding the temple as cover. The Order of the Black Sun probably hadn't expected that their vehicles would be used as a fairly decent shroud for three of their escaped prisoners to use.

Nina scanned the surroundings, being sure to check to see if there were any sentries standing guard besides the ones that Elijah was distracting. Every so often, she would glance back at Elijah to check how he was doing. As they got close to the temple entrance, she looked back and saw a much less civilized conversation happening.

Elijah threw himself onto one of the men he was speaking with and threw another hard right hook into the man's face. Just like Marco back at the facility, it was a good punch that knocked out the sentry with one hit. The second guard though, moved to gun Elijah down. She heard muffled shouts from that distance but just enough to make out the words. "What the hell are you doing--"

Before the guard could open fire, Elijah had tackled that guard into the snow too. For someone who was very humble about his fighting abilities and who admitted that he was very inexperienced in combat, Elijah had a talent for fighting dirty and knocking people out. His form could use some work and he rolled off of his opponents, prying their guns out of their holsters. He came marching toward the temple where the others were, looking embarrassed. He straightened his glasses which had nearly been knocked off his face in the struggle.

"You saw that?"

"I saw that..." Nina said awkwardly. "It was a good fight."

"I surprise myself sometimes," Elijah said. "Here." He handed one of the guns to Nina and the other to Jean. "Fists are one thing. You really don't want me shooting a gun. We'll all be dead within minutes."

"I'll take your word for it," Nina said. She didn't have a huge amount of experience with firearms either but she had enough to know not to accidentally riddle everyone in sight with bullets. "Let's go. We can't let Julian figure out how the altar works. If he does...then we might be in a very bad situation."

THEY ENTERED the temple and were met by a number of light fixtures illuminating the whole place. The Black Sun had certainly done a good job making sure they could see inside of such a dreary place. But it also gave them less cover to work with when sneaking around. There were a few different corridors that could take, but if they wanted to find the altar, the best move might be to split up.

"Elijah, you and I will take this corridor. Jean and Charles, you go left." She dictated the plan without any hesitation. All she cared about now was getting the job done. They had their chance to leave and flee far away from the Order of the Black Sun, but now that they were here, they needed to settle all of this once and for all. The others followed her plan and got moving. Each pair had at least one person with a gun in case they ran into any trouble. Hopefully, they wouldn't bump into anyone too dangerous.

Almost as she had the thought, they heard three gunshots ring out behind them, echoing through the hall and bouncing through the temple. It had to be Jean and Charles. They might still be alive but those gunshots had no doubt alerted every single one of the Black Sun operatives that were stationed within the temple. Elijah moved to fall back and Nina caught his arm before he could leave. "Where are you going?"

"I'll check on them. You go on ahead."

Elijah didn't let her argue the point. He broke free of her grip and ran back down the halls. She had to press on. Hopefully the altar wasn't too far away. Even if she could just break it somehow, that would stop Julian from being able to use it. There were more gunshots behind her but she had to ignore it. Whatever was happening, she just hoped that those gun shots weren't killing her friends.

Nina rounded the corner and found herself face to face with Julian Corvus. He froze and those icy gray eyes of his grew large. Usually he was so scarily calm but now...now he looked genuinely surprised.

"Dr. Gould...how did you--"

Nina didn't hesitate and had the upper hand. She expected him to be here. Julian was still reeling from seeing her and she took full advantage of that surprise. Nina fired a whole clip of bullets into Julian's face, causing him to stagger backward. It wouldn't kill him but it would delay him long enough for her to get by. He held his hands over his bloody face but she knew whatever wounds she'd inflicted wouldn't last long. His immortality was probably already patching them up. She took the chance to sprint past him down a narrow dark corridor until she found herself in a large chamber.

A stone table stood in the center of the room and she recognized Purdue sprawled atop it on his back. Nearby, Sam Cleave was tied to a pillar. Sam saw her first, and his mouth fell open.

"Nina?"

"Nina? Where?" Purdue cried out, trying to shuffle his head around enough to see.

"It's me," Nina said, rushing forward.

Purdue couldn't believe what he was seeing when she appeared over him. He blinked hard, like she would suddenly disappear when he opened his eyes back up but she remained. "We were trying to save you."

"Beat you to it," Nina said with a smile. "Now I'm the one that has to save you slow bastards."

The second Purdue was broken free, Nina threw her arms around him and hugged him tight. She did the same with Sam when he cut free from the pillar. She never thought she was see either of them ever again. It didn't feel real and she was scared that they would turn to dust in her arms. She really hoped this was real.

Julian appeared behind them. There were no bullet sized crater in his face, no sign at all that he had been shot. “Well...look at this. The gang back together. Reunited. It's almost heartwarming to see but mostly...it's just a reminder that I've let this go on far too long. I should have just killed you, Dr. Gould. How did you even get out?”

“I had help,” Nina said defiantly. “You're not nearly as loved by the order as you think you are.”

Julian tightened his tie and brushed off his suit. “That will change today. When I ensure that the Order of the Black Sun gets everything.”

“Yeah, that's not going to happen.”

Elijah, Jean, and Charles entered the chamber. Jean had Mona Greer's book of shadows in his hands and Charles had palmed the pearl that could control the ocean. Whatever fight they had gotten into in the halls had ended with them reclaiming those items from the Black Sun. That was much better than them being dead. They looked more than ready for a fight, and now they had the numbers.

“First Sasha conspires against me...now you, Mr. Dane. How very disappointing. Is there really so little loyalty within the Order of the Black Sun?”

Elijah pushed his glasses up the ridge of his nose. “There is when there's someone like you running things. Some leaders don't deserve loyalty.”

“We gave you everything you wanted. Relics to study. A place to live--”

"I was still a prisoner," Elijah said sharply and glanced at Nina. "You just dressed it up differently. It took me awhile to see that. But my vision's never been the best."

"We were all prisoners," Jean-Luc said, the book of shadows opened. "But not anymore."

Julian didn't look worried at all about their presence. If anything, he looked excited to get to face them. "Is that old witch's diary supposed to scare me? It really doesn't."

"In the hands of an amateur like Purdue, maybe not. But I've spent years studying the craft. I know how to make it hurt."

Julian laughed. "So what? Magic or no magic, I can't be killed."

"You will wish you could be."

Jean held out his hand and started reading from the book, the words barely sounded like they came from any language at all. They oozed and unfurled from his lips like it took all of his strength to speak them.

Julian went to reach for the book, to try and pry it out of Jean's hands but he suddenly recoiled and stopped, struck by an unseen force. He was quivering and looked paralyzed. All he could manage was a groan of pain and blood started seeping down from his eye sockets, his nose, his mouth, and even his ears. He tried to move but his body was frozen in place. The spell Jean cast had taken hold of him, restraining all of his movement and tearing away at his insides.

Purdue knew that the book of shadows was filled with all kinds of brutal spells. The contents of the tome had supposedly driven previous readers mad. The things inside those pages had made someone as notoriously optimistic as David Purdue act with extreme caution in his handling of it, and had kept it from daring to read most of it.

Jean-Luc Gerard had spent years reading all kinds of grimoires. If anyone could handle reading from Mona Greer's manuscript, it was him.

Julian hissed as more of his insides streamed out of him. Cuts started forming across his body like an invisible scalpel was slashing away at him. Thanks to his regenerative power, the cuts were healing themselves soon after they appeared but more kept coming. He may have been immortal, but he could still feel pain.

"You must have enjoyed keeping me prisoner...I barely had anything to do with your fight with Purdue. I barely knew the man, but you took me hostage anyway just because I was having dinner at his house. You didn't need to do that. I wasn't his friend. I was an associate at best. But you just wanted to hurt as many people as you could. You're going to regret having ever done that."

Julian stumbled backward, holding his head as Jean-Luc chanted a new incantation that seemed to be melting Julian's brain, from what Purdue could surmise. Who knew what other warped things that the magic from that book could do to him.

"Your book store will burn!" Julian screamed as he held his skull. "All of it."

"No it won't," Jean said calmly and started speaking new words. Julian was lifted off of his feet, levitating into the air and was suddenly thrown hard against the wall, pinned there by some invisible force. He was still screaming in pain. "No, you're done hurting anyone."

The power coming from that old book emanated throughout the room. The cruelty and malice of its original author practically oozed off the pages and seeped onto the floor. Purdue could just imagine that witch, Mona Greer, reciting those same spells and watching her victims be completely eviscerated like Julian would have been if not for his own power. Those chilling and forbidden sounds that Jean-Luc read so perfectly probably hadn't been spoken since they left Mona Greer's lips hundreds of years ago. It was almost like she was in the room, and that made Purdue extremely uncomfortable, but he was grateful that her magic was doing so much damage to Julian.

Blood started running down from Jean's left eye as he kept reading and performing the spell. The book's contents were even taking a toll on him but he was doing far better than anyone else could have in that position.

Jean seemed to notice the ill effects that were taking place and he wiped the blood off his cheek with his free hand before screaming a new spell and Julian's neck suddenly snapped violently. The

Black Sun's leader slid down the wall to the floor as Jean closed the book. It wasn't enough to kill him but snapping his neck would at least take him out of commission for a bit until his body inevitably mended itself.

Nina couldn't believe what she was seeing. They were actually winning this battle.

14

CHAPTER FOURTEEN - THE LOVELESS GIRL

Kendra bolted out of the room and Sam immediately took off after her. He didn't want to leave the others behind with Julian but at the same time, he needed to sort out his own private issues that were happening inside of this temple. He needed to get to the bottom of everything with Kendra, and find out where they really stood.

"Kendra stop!"

She was bounding up old narrow steps upward and Sam kept close behind. The temple was a tall structure and there were many steps to take but they kept ascending until they came to an opening that brought them to the very top of the temple, suddenly being bathed in sunlight. Kendra glanced back at him but didn't otherwise acknowledge him, running across the black rooftop, like there was no way she would ever be caught.

Kendra came to the edge of the roof and looked

over the edge. It was a long way down and she turned around to face her ex-lover. She had a knife held tightly in her grip, waving it at Sam threateningly.

"Well this is romantic, isn't it, Sam? This view is breathtaking. Is that why you followed me? You wanted one last date, is that it?"

"Not especially, no," Sam said honestly. "Frankly, I think this might be a good time to tell you that we're through. I'm breaking up with you officially as of this moment. It wasn't working between us, and if I'm going to be truthful, I could probably do a lot better than you."

Kendra looked stunned by his words. Obviously he was playing a little coy and sarcastic but she seemed to really be taking it to heart. But that moment of strange pain was replaced by more of her ugly laughing.

"Oh, how will I ever recover!?"

Sam still hadn't come to terms with what Kendra actually was, but it helped when she was standing right in front of him, no longer hiding behind her act. He could see her real face, the one that filled him with so much anger. She had played him, completely manipulated him.

Nina was suddenly by his side, having followed him up to the roof, and gently touched his hand. "You okay? Everything good?"

"I'm good," Sam said.

"So is this your new girlfriend then?" Kendra cackled. "You got over me that easily? Or were you seeing her the whole time? Keeping secrets, Sammy. That's not good for any healthy relationship. Love requires trust and honesty, doesn't it? I think so."

The real Kendra wasn't the sweet, supportive, and empathetic girl that he thought he was sleeping beside all of those nights. No, she was a disgusting creature that loved to play psychological warfare. She loved playing mind games, that's all it ever was to her. A turn of a game, and she was just waiting for the next roll of the dice to see if she could start playing for real—and she was. This was the real Kendra, and he hated her with every fiber of his being.

"You know how good Sammy is in the sack, right?" Kendra laughed, addressing Nina. "Don't you? I heard conflicting things about your relationship. He and I, though, there was no conflict about it. He was loving every second he was with me. I think he might have even been falling in love."

"Get over yourself," Sam said, but the sting of her words wasn't entirely without truth. "You're just like all of the other Black Sun cronies. Sad people who joined that cult just to feel like they had a purpose in life."

"So what are you going to do then, Sam? Kill me? That doesn't seem like you at all. You were so gentle. That's what you are. Your hands are soft and so are those lips. You couldn't hurt me even if you wanted to. No. You're going to tell me off and try and convince yourself that you hate me, but you still want me even now. You're probably hoping this is all some sort of trick or a bad dream."

"You're making a lot of assumptions about me...all of which are wrong. You spend a little while in my bed and act like you and I have known each other for years."

He took a step forward and Kendra glanced down over the edge of the temple, contemplating if she could maybe slide down it or even survive the fall. She was in a corner now. All she had left was trying to play her little head games.

"You don't know me, Kendra. I've been through hell for years. The only things that have kept me upright and still functioning were my friends. I was in a very bad place. I could have gone looking for purpose like you have, joined some ass hat secret society of lunatics like you did, but instead I toughed it out and stayed true to myself, until real friends and real purpose came along."

Kendra just broke down laughing. "Do you have any idea how pathetic that sounds? All of that nonsense about having a good heart and staying true to one's self. You read that shit in some self-help book, Sammy? No, life is about opportunities. People are either brave enough to take them, or they aren't. You want to stay true to yourself, good, but the only way to do that is to accept that you can only rely on yourself. There is no we. There is no us. Relationships are garbage lies where two people convince themselves that they need the other. No.

It's all lies. People are much, much better off on their own. With themselves. Just themselves!"

"Do you seem better off right now?" Nina cut in, acknowledging that Kendra was standing on the edge of a long fall while she and Sam had the advantage. "Because it doesn't look like you are. The order you joined aren't going to try to help you because all of them are just like you. They all think about themselves, and only themselves first. So congratulations. You're on your own, just like you wanted. So show us how powerful being on your own makes you then."

"Shut up you tramp!" Kendra snapped. "You all are going to lose!"

"No we're not," Sam said. "We're stopping the Order of the Black Sun right now. Just like we always have. Your boss got a few good licks in, I'll give him that. But because we've stuck together, even when we were across the world from each other, we're going to pull out a win."

Sam took a step forward toward Kendra and she waved the knife around again. "Stay back! Stay back!"

Sam raised his arms in surrender. "I'm not going to hurt you, Kendra. I should, but I won't. Just throw the knife off the edge, and step away. We're not going to kill you."

"You want to, though! You want to!"

Kendra was sounding crazed now, a far cry from the sweet woman who always gave him such helpful and wise advice in those late hours of the night before bed. Tears rolled down her face and he saw that she was starting to break. Everything that she was, all of those lies and deceptions, was worthless now that the truth was out and she wasn't going to win. That sweet and beautiful facade she wore was gone and now even the face beneath that was peeling away.

"I...I don't know who I really am, Sam. I don't I couldn't tell you my favorite color or my favorite food. I'm not even sure if I have one...I couldn't tell you anything personal about me because there is no me! Not really. I could tell you the things about the girl I was with you. That girl you so stupidly fell for. But she's not me. She never was. And I don't...there are so many times when I look at myself in the mirror and I have no idea who I am seeing. There have been so many girls with this face. Nice girls. Mean girls. Patient girls. Stubborn girls. Smart girls. Dumb girls. So, so many wonderful young women to give life to. They're all so different. I made them...they're...I...they're all so unique. But one thing I can tell you, yes one thing I can tell you...is that all of those beautiful girls are liars. All of them. They're all liars. They're not as real as they want you to think!"

It was killing Sam to have to see this disturbed human being that had played her tricks on him. It was still hard to believe that she was even the same woman that he had loved spending time with. It was all fake, everything about her, and now she was realizing it too. Kendra had never had a real life, she just lived tons of other lives and none of them were real either.

She was gasping for air, trying to catch her breath in her hysteria but she wasn't calming down. She was looking back and forth from Sam to the edge of the temple's roof.

"You have your own wants! Don't you!? Your own personality! Your own identity! I don't! I never have! I'm not a person at all. I'm just a piece of many different ones! I loved it for a while but now...now I wish I had something, anything at all, for myself! But I don't! I never will because there is no me at all! There is no mine. There is no myself. And there is no us! There never was! Stop looking at me like I'm here! I'm not!"

"Calm down, Kendra," Sam said. "So you wanted the Order of the Black Sun to give you more roles to play and you thought that...what...eventually one of those roles would stick? Or that maybe if you kept piecing together different people, at some point you would have enough knowledge to stitch up your own? That's not how it works. That's not how any of it works. Life isn't about playing a role. It's about being true to yourself and what you want out of it--"

"True to myself!? Have you been listening to anything I've been saying!? There is nothing for me to be true to? Which self should I be true to? The girl that you loved? Is that what you want!?"

"No..." Sam said and dared to move a little closer, much to Kendra's fury.

"Stay away! You're lying! You're going to kill me!"

"I'm not lying," Sam said, taking another cautious step. "That's not my way. That's Julian's way. We're not the Black Sun, Kendra. We're not. You chose the wrong side but we can get you help, make sure that no one else needs to get hurt."

"Or I could gut you!" Kendra suddenly hissed.

"You could, yes, but what exactly would that accomplish?"

Kendra slashed her knife through the air and Sam stopped his approach. He could probably disarm her but on the edge like that, it was too risky. She was wild right now, and reasoning wasn't helping anything. In her thrashing, Kendra swung too hard and her foot slipped. She careened backwards toward open air, off the temple roof.

Sam ran forward and caught hold of her as she hung off the side. He clung onto her free hand while the other dangled away, still holding the knife. She was sobbing hysterically, gasping so hard that she couldn't even catch her own breath.

"Don't love me, Sam."

"I don't," Sam said bluntly, still trying to reel the rest of her in. "Trust me. You've proven that you are definitely not my type."

"I don't love you...I don't love anyone, really. I don't why. I just never have. Ever. Not my family. Not all of the boys that threw themselves at me every chance they had. I just felt...empty all the time. All the time. All the time. All the time..."

She was trailing off, lost in her own ramblings.

Sam tried to pull her back to the roof but she seemed to be pulling her own body weight in the opposite direction. "What the hell are you doing?"

"Why don't I love anyone!?" She shrieked loudly and suddenly.

Her eyes went wide with mania and she swiped at him with the knife in her other hand. The blade grazed Sam's arm and he instinctively pulled back, releasing her. Kendra screamed and fell from the top of the temple, crashing down to the earth far below.

Sam stood and peered over the edge, holding the scratch on his arm. He was glad that the knife hadn't found some place more vital in her attack, but felt some sadness that he hadn't been able to keep her from dying. A hand touched his shoulder and Nina stood beside him.

"There was nothing we could do. She was far too gone...honestly I don't think she was ever really here at all. She just had to act like she was. Couldn't have been easy."

"This whole trip, I thought I would be seeing her sleeping in my bed when I got back. That's definitely not happening...it still doesn't feel like the same person. Like...maybe she is still back there. The Kendra I knew."

"She's not," Nina said bluntly. "This was her. The real her. And frankly, you have terrible taste in women."

15

CHAPTER FIFTEEN - THE SACRIFICE AND THE SERVANT

The sacrificial chamber had become a battleground.

Black Sun agents poured into the chamber. Julian might have been knocked unconscious but his commands were obviously still being carried out—and those commands involved killing the people trying to bring the order down. All of the operatives were armed and were being led by that buffoon Boris. Boris raised his gun to shoot at Jean but Jean was already finishing an incantation for one of the book of shadows' spells. Boris' body popped like a balloon and his leftovers splashed all over his comrades.

Purdue felt a bit jealous that Jean got to use the spell that he wanted to use on Boris. That should have been Purdue casting that spell but unfortunately, he was awful and scared of that magic. Jean made it look easy. Purdue would have probably just accidentally killed himself with that particular spell.

There were too many Black Sun agents though and many just ignored Jean, who was still trying to stop more of them with magic. They all raised their weapons and those guns were pointed at Purdue. Evidently, even the lowest of the order knew who he was and that if they had to kill someone, it should be Purdue. He stared straight down the many barrels of those weapons

The Black Sun operatives opened fired and Purdue braced himself. The bullets never reached him. Charles had stepped in front of him, forming a human barrier and shielded Purdue from the gunfire. Purdue let out a yell of concern as Jean-Luc disarmed the guards with another spell. Purdue expected the old man to be on the floor riddled with bullets, but he was still standing. When Purdue stepped in front of him to examine him, he found that the holes in Charles' body were mending themselves. It was just like with Julian's own body.

"What...?"

"It has been quite some time indeed, sir," Charles said bashfully. "You have missed some things since our separation. That monster, Julian Corvus, tested that spear of his on me. He wanted to know if his immortality was a one-time occurrence or if the spear really could bestow everlasting life. As you can see...when he stabbed me with it...he learned that it could give anyone that power."

"You're immortal?" Purdue could hardly believe it. Charles had always been a good ally to have at his side but he was just his butler, and now he was one of the two people on the planet that couldn't be killed and might even live forever. "You?"

"Yes, sir," Charles said with a little smile. "It seems I will be serving your house for some time to come. So you best start having some children."

"Unlikely," Purdue said and pulled his butler into a hug. "I'm just glad you're not dead."

"He never will be," Jean said beside them. "But we're not as invulnerable, are we? We need to get the hell out of here. Now."

Something struck Jean hard from behind and knocked him onto the floor, unconscious. Julian stood over him, having gotten up from the floor, shaking off whatever painful hex had been crippling him on the floor. He looked more than furious—he wanted to rip all of them into tiny little pieces and make it as painful as possible.

"Get back to the altar. You will be sacrificed," Julian hissed.

"You could have just killed anyone to get your wish," Purdue said with a shrug. "You just had to make it personal. This vendetta you have got in the way of getting whatever wish you wanted granted. That's just a bit pathetic, aye? It's over, Julian. Enough of this."

"It's not over at all. You haven't won anything."

Charles took a protective step in front of Purdue. Purdue would usually never have wanted his old butler to try and fight for him, but he knew now that Charles had a far better chance than he did. He had the same power as Julian, so would actually be able to put up a fight. Two immortal beings—it could be a very long fight.

"I should never have tested the spear on you," Julian growled. "Honestly, I was hoping you would stay dead. Not only would that assure me that I'm the only one who should have this gift...but it would also have been a nice thing to throw in Purdue's face."

"If you didn't want to be immortal, then you shouldn't have even stabbed me with the spear. A truly foolish gambit, sir. And now you have to deal with the consequences."

"Consequences?" Julian laughed. "What consequences? Immortality or not, you're still a fragile old man. You won't suddenly be able to beat me in a fight, you know that right? All it will do will make it easier for me to beat you for even longer."

Charles surprisingly waved Julian on, taunting him to come at him. Suddenly, Purdue wasn't looking at an older man that usually just cleaned his house, served him food, and drove him around. No, now he was seeing a true friend and ally standing up against one of their greatest enemies. Charles had lost almost just as much to the Black Sun as Purdue had. He'd lost the house that he took care of, his own freedom when he was taken prisoner, and apparently even his normal life during those experiments that Julian performed on him with the holy lance. He wanted to win this fight too, and for a moment, Purdue really believed that the old man could.

Julian's surprise was apparent. He obviously didn't expect Charles to be much of anything, certainly not a threat. But now he saw that the butler was serious about taking him on.

“No matter.” Julian picked up the Spear of Destiny from the floor. “It seems this spear gave you more than everlasting life. It gave you a spine, maybe a little bit of youth, hm? Interesting. It really is full of surprises, isn't it? I was shocked when it brought me back from death. Try to imagine it, waking up with this thing sticking out of your heart. Yes, it's full of surprises, but I'm not fond of surprises. So I've been studying it constantly since taking it out of my body. In that research, you were nothing more than a lab rat, that was all. But contrary to what you believe, you were not the only one that I tested it on.”

Julian raised the spear's tip in front of his face and flashed a huge Cheshire grin.

“No. After my test worked on you, I plunged this spear into two others' chests. Two workers of mine. They were incompetent and most of all, expendable. Just like you and me, they were given immortality...but then I had another idea...I stabbed them each again after their resurrections. This time, they didn't heal...they stayed dead for good.

You see, we aren't entirely invulnerable. Like all things, we have a weakness. The Spear of Destiny may have blessed us with eternal life...but it can also take it away."

Purdue couldn't believe what he was hearing. The Spear of Destiny could actually kill someone who had been given its power. It could actually slay someone who was otherwise immortal—someone like Julian. Julian had made a far bigger mistake than he realized, bringing the one thing that could hurt him with him on this mission, and Purdue was going to make sure that he paid for that mistake dearly. He would make sure that the spear found its way into Julian's heart.

Before he could even begin to think of a way to get that spear from Julian and turn it on him, the Order of the Black Sun's leader was advancing on Charles. Suddenly, Purdue realized that the situation was much more precarious than he thought. If it could kill Julian, then it could kill anyone else who also shared his immortality—and that included his butler.

"So, as you can see, there's only one way we can really settle this conundrum."

Charles stood his ground but even with all of his stubborn desires to protect Purdue, he was looking nervous now too.

Julian rushed Charles, charging at him with the spear held out in front of him.

Purdue wanted to jump in the way. At least if he got stabbed by the Spear of Destiny, then he would be given its power. If Charles was stabbed, then that would it for him. It would actually kill him for good.

But he couldn't move quick enough.

Charles tried to get out of the way but Julian moved with too much agility. The Spear of Destiny's blade found its mark in the old butler's chest. Julian speared Charles like a fish and drove the holy lance deep into the man's chest. He skewered him, continuing his run forward until he pushed the impaled butler onto the altar at the center of the chamber.

Charles let out a gasp as all of the air was sucked out of him, his immortal life spilling out into the air. He crashed hard onto the altar, wincing and groaning from the sudden attack. Purdue let out a roar and went to run at Julian but his body froze as he realized just how bad the situation was. Charles was dying on the sacred altar, his blood spilling out onto the stone slab just as the Black Sun planned to happen to Purdue.

Purdue couldn't move. He was trembling at the sight of Julian completing his objective. A man was dying at the altar, being offered as a sacrifice for Julian to make his wish. It was over. After everything he'd been through to reclaim his life from the Order of the Black Sun, they still won. He still couldn't beat them even after getting so close.

"You weren't my ideal choice," Julian hissed down at the dying man, still pushing the shaft of the spear into him. "But you will make for a fine sacrifice nonetheless." Julian's head craned to his right to stare at the dumbstruck Purdue. "I actually prefer this. You get to watch such an old friend die and I get my wish...and I can promise you, Mr. Purdue, my wish is going to include a fate far worse than death for you."

Purdue took a clumsy step forward, reaching for Charles who was gasping and bleeding on the altar. The butler reached out for Purdue, choking on his own blood. Charles had always been there for him, always there to support all of his ventures. And even on the quiet days, was there to help him with whatever he needed. He was one of his best friends, but so often he treated him like he was just a servant.

"Charles...I..."

It was too late.

The light left Charles' eyes as he tried to speak. The man who had been so supportive of him through all of his obsessive adventures was gone and his death was going to be used as an engine for the Order of the Black Sun to win. His body was being desecrated and his memory defiled so that Julian Corvus could get everything he wanted. It wasn't fair. None of it was fair.

Julian was going to get his wish.

No. Purdue wouldn't let him, not after all of this. That bastard didn't deserve to win. The Order of the Black Sun wouldn't leave victorious. There had to be a way.

Purdue let out a primal roar and charged Julian,

tackling him onto the floor. Julian snarled at him like a beast and smashed his head against Purdue's, throwing him off of him. Purdue wouldn't give up and was pouncing on him seconds later. He couldn't give up. He wouldn't.

As they grappled on the floor, Julian cackled.

"It's too late! It's too late you stupid fool! Your butler is dead! The sacrifice is made! I wish--"

Before the wish could be spoken aloud, Purdue smashed his knuckles against Julian's jaw. Maybe he couldn't voice his desire with a broken jaw. He punched him again and again but Julian just kept laughing through the blood in his mouth and the bruises that were being made instantly faded away. Julian's immortality just added to the futility of Purdue's attempts. There was no way to stop him. Not unless he had the Spear of Destiny.

Julian threw Purdue off, climbing to his feet and rushed over to the sacred alta. He stood proudly over the slab and Charles' body.

"Purdue!" Nina called as she and Sam sprinted back into the chamber.

Purdue was getting up off the floor and even across the room, he saw the terror in his friends' eyes. They were realizing, just as he had, that they had truly lost this time. There wouldn't be any coming back from whatever horrors Julian Corvus had in mind for the future. They would be at the mercy of that sadist's vile imagination.

Part of Purdue was glad that the three of them were together again, here at the end. If anyone was going to be at his side for this defeat, it would be his two companions. They'd been through so many adventures together, gone all over the world. Through all of it, all of those close encounters with death, they'd always come out on top. Their luck had run out though, and now they would have to get through this together too, in whatever way they could.

Julian was still spewing out that demented laugh, not being able to contain the glee he was feeling. He must have felt so good, now that he was at the brink of world conquest and undeniable victory.

“I'm glad you're all here to see this,” Julian said with a giggle. “I'm so, so glad.” Julian turned his attention back to the bloody altar. He looked like a child on Christmas morning, ready to see all of the great things that he would be unwrapping, only he was about to see the world that he always wanted come to fruition. “I wish...”

Purdue, Nina, and Sam all ran forward but they would never get there in time.

It was over.

“I wish to be the god of this world!”

The three of them all came to a skittering stop.

The wish was made.

Purdue half-expected the world to instantly change around them, to see the horrors that no doubt flooded Julian Corvus's mind. With him as a god, the planet would become nothing more than a hellscape with Julian ruling unchallenged over everyone.

Julian stood, with his arms outstretched, waiting to be bestowed his newfound omnipotence. They all watched, waiting for something to happen, but nothing ever did. Nothing about him changed, at least noticeably.

Sam took a cautious step forward. “So? Do you feel like a god?”

Julian looked himself over uncertainly. He looked around, also waiting for some kind of sign that he was now a deity but there was no bright flash of light, or lightning bolt coming to wrap around his hands. He wasn't glowing. He was just him, the same as he had always been.

“I wish to be a god!” He repeated, more loudly and more forcefully, hoping to convince whatever unseen force to give him the wish that he had been promised.

Again, nothing happened.

“Oh my god...” Nina said, and she started smiling.

“It didn't work,” Sam said, also looking elated. “It didn't work!”

Julian kept examining his hands and then looking back at all of the blood on the altar. He was reeling, probably scrambling to figure out why he hadn't gotten what he wanted. Everything that he had heard and learned told him that his wish would be granted, but something was still preventing him from finally claiming his dreams.

"I wish to be a god!" He screeched again, far more uneasily this time. He was desperate now, practically begging the alta to give him what he wanted. "That's my wish! Make me a god of this world!"

Purdue stepped up beside Nina and Sam. The three of them watched Julian struggle and all of them felt a tinge of satisfaction seeing him having so little control over the situation he found himself in. He was a child throwing a temper tantrum now, furious that things weren't going to end up going his way.

"So that's it?" Purdue asked. "The story about this place was wrong? Just a bunch of bullshit, aye? The sacrifice at the altar didn't work."

"Seems so," Sam said with a sigh of relief.

"No," Nina said, shocking both Purdue and Sam. "No, the sacrifice worked. Just not the way that any of us expected it to. Look at Charles."

Charles was still motionless and bloody on top of the slab of rock but there was a glass of wine and a book resting beside where his hand hung. Those hadn't been there before, and Purdue looked at the book cover closely. It was Twenty Thousand Leagues Under the Sea by Jules Verne, which he had known for years was Charles' favorite novel of all time.

"What the...?"

Nina gave a little laugh, practically coughing on her own surprise. "Elijah told me something about the temple, an old legend he had heard about it during all of his time curating and studying history. He said that everyone was saying that if you perform a sacrifice at the altar, you get whatever you want, but he had actually heard the opposite."

"What do you mean exactly?"

"I mean that it was never about the person performing the sacrifice. It was about the sacrifice themselves. The one who was given their heart's desire had to give up their own heart. They had to sacrifice themselves to acquire what they were looking for. Julian didn't get what he wanted because he wasn't the sacrifice, Charles was."

Julian looked over at them, having overheard her story. He looked dazed, and even a little crazed. "Speak up! What are you talking about?"

"I'm saying that you didn't get your wish. You were never going to. The sacrifice was the only one who would get what they wanted. You didn't get what you wanted but Charles did."

"A book and a drink?" Sam asked.

"He said it on the way here. He didn't want to come initially. He just wanted to be back home with a good book and a drink. It's what he wanted, but we were able to convince him to come to help you, Purdue."

Purdue couldn't help but feel a little guilty but thankfully that was drowned out by the feeling that they hadn't actually lost after all. They won in the end thanks to Julian Corvus not knowing everything about the Mayan temple.

"You're wrong!" Julian spat venomously.

"Am I? Then explain Twenty Thousand Leagues Under the Sea and his favorite glass of red wine right there."

Julian glanced at the two items beside the dead butler's hand. They had been conjured from nowhere, a gift in exchange for the sacrifice that had been made.

Nina spoke up, relishing having the advantage over Julian. "The only way you could ever get what you want would be to sacrifice yourself on that alta...but seeing as how you're immortal, that doesn't seem possible."

But it was possible, at least Julian and Purdue now knew that. Purdue looked at the Spear of Destiny protruding from the butler's corpse and the same idea crossed their minds simultaneously. All Julian had to do was stab himself with the spear on the alta and could make his wish. It was a risk but if he wished for godhood then perhaps that would counteract his death, bringing him back an omnipotent entity just like he wanted.

"Don't let him use the spear!" Purdue yelled, already rushing forward.

Julian grabbed the shaft of the Spear of Destiny and tried to pry it out of Charles' body. It didn't slide out as easily as he hoped, stuck in his torso. Purdue led the charge toward him. Nina and Sam were probably confused but he hoped they believed in him enough to follow. Julian used both hands to heave the Spear of Destiny out of Charles and prepared to turn it on himself.

Purdue threw himself at Julian, putting his own hands on the shaft of the spear and trying to pull it away from his enemy's grip. Julian wasn't letting go, though. They struggled for the spear until Sam and Nina got to Purdue's side. Sam grabbed onto Julian from behind, trying to pull him away from Purdue and the spear while Nina tried to help Purdue with the tug of war for the weapon.

They managed to knock the spear away and it skittered across the floor. Before Julian could try and reclaim it, Purdue and Sam grabbed onto both of his arms. Purdue kicked the back of his leg and Julian fell to his knees, completely restrained by the two men. Nina ran after the spear and picked it up. They dragged Julian across the floor, further away from the alta.

"The spear can take away the immortality that it gave," Purdue explained as he struggled to keep Julian down. "That's how he killed Charles."

"So he was trying to kill himself to perform another sacrifice," Nina said, looking over the spear in her hands. She looked sickened by the sight of Charles' blood running down it, still fresh. She walked up to Julian and stood over him with the spear. She put the tip of the spear up to Julian's neck, letting the blade poke at his throat. "Do you remember the last time I held this."

Julian stopped struggling, completely bound by Purdue and Sam's hold on him. He looked at the spear and then up at Nina. An uncomfortable little smile formed on his face. He was fuming, but he probably thought that there was still a chance.

"I do," Julian said coldly. "When you drove it through me in that cave. When I thought I was going to die."

"When you should have died," Nina corrected. "You were just lucky that this spear could help you cheat death...but it seems it can also put you down for good, is that right?"

"It is," Julian said expectantly. "So this is your big moment then? You're going to finish what you started all of that time ago, is that it? Go on then, Dr. Gould. You had your chance before. You took your shot. You can take it again. It's only fitting."

"Nina," Purdue said. "Wait."

Nina pressed the spear a little harder against Julian's throat. She wanted to run him through with it, just as she had before. This time, he would really be gone. He wouldn't be coming back. She would finally have slain the beast that had been haunting her ever since. All of the horrible things that had come all because that spear hadn't worked the way it should have the first time...all because she hadn't been able to get rid of Julian Corvus for good.

The attacks on her life and her friends. Her imprisonment and torture in that dark little cell in the Black Sun facility. All of the pain that had come was because she couldn't make sure that the spear put him down permanently. The Order of the Black Sun had only grown far worse since her failed attempt to kill Julian.

Everything started at that moment, when she ran him through with it. It had seemed like such a triumph at the time. She had beaten the bad guy. But it had all been some cruel joke that fate was playing on her. Julian came back.

Charles was dead now because of the effects of that moment.

And now she had that power in her hands once again, and she could put an end to Julian Corvus. She wanted to do it more than anything, to take back the victory that should have been hers but Julian had taken away.

"Nina..." Purdue said again.

Why was Purdue telling her to wait? He wanted Julian gone just as much as she did, surely. They needed to wipe this stain off the face of the earth for good. It was their responsibility to ensure that the Order of the Black Sun stopped desecrating history and threatening the future. Getting rid of their most dangerous leader was a great way to start fixing the mistakes they had made—the mistakes she made. This was their chance.

"You want to," Julian cooed. "You should."

"Nina, we're too close to the altar. Even here." Purdue pointed at the alta a few yards away. "We don't know for certain that blood being spilled this close won't activate the sacrifice. We can't risk it."

"Then let's bring him outside...we can finish this there." Nina was surprised by her own coldness but that was the effect that this terrible man had on her. He had tormented her for far too long. She hated the idea that he was going to be able to leave this room alive. He deserved to be put down and purged from the world. The planet would be a lot safer of a place without him. "We have to kill him."

"No we don't," Purdue said. Nina glared at Purdue but Purdue just shook his head. "We can't decide that here. We can talk about it later. But listen to me, we can't risk killing anyone in here. You're right about the sacrifice...we have to make sure everyone leaves this place breathing. We can't have anyone else's wishes coming true. They won't be nearly as harmless as Charles's was, aye?"

Nina considered just doing it. Who was Purdue to try and stop her? He didn't have a clue what she had been through since they parted ways. He didn't know what it was like to be under the Order of the Black Sun's thumb, at Julian's mercy for so long. He didn't know about that darkness.

Then again, she didn't know what Purdue had been through either...not fully. But she knew enough to realize that Purdue had suffered just as much if not more than she had, just maybe in different ways. But at least she probably still had a home to go back to, and had heirlooms and belongings that hadn't been stripped from a destroyed house. She may have been taken prisoner, but Purdue lost everything thanks to Julian. In the end, maybe he did have a right to decide what happened to their mutual bane.

"Okay..."

Nina lowered the Spear of Destiny, pulling the tip away from Julian's throat. As much as she wanted to try and kill him again—and this time succeed—she shouldn't make that choice on her own. They had all been through hell thanks to Julian's rise of power. Ever since he'd come into their lives, things had gotten so much harder. It should be a group decision, not just hers. Part of her still wished she had gotten what she wanted but she knew it was a selfish wish. Julian wasn't just her enemy. He was all of theirs.

But she couldn't stand looking at him, especially as he now smiled up at her.

"I'm disappointed, Dr. Gould."

"I don't care."

There was a sound like cracking earth, and the stone walls of the chamber started to tremble. Purdue recognized those tremors well enough. It was just like it had been standing outside of the temple in Honduras. The Mayan temple was preparing to teleport to a new location. Any second now, they could be anywhere on Earth. It could be hundreds of miles away or even thousands. It could be some place warmer or somewhere even colder. There was no way to tell, but Purdue knew it was coming at any moment.

"What's going on?" Nina asked, dropped the Spear of Destiny when the floor rattled beneath her. The holy lance slid across the floor. "What's happening?"

"The temple is moving again, right?" Sam asked

beside Purdue, who just nodded back at him in response.

Julian started laughing in their grip, like he was about to witness the biggest firework show that was ever launched. He kept gazing around at each of the walls around them and then at the floor, hoping to see the first sign that they were being moved.

"This is interesting, isn't it? It's one thing to hear about the temple moving or to be just outside of it as it vanishes, right, Mr. Purdue? But to actually be inside...to move with it. To be in one place and then instantly in another...that's something special. My apologies, Dr. Gould. I would have hated if you killed me and I had to miss this spectacle. That would have been a terrible waste."

Nina ignored his taunts as the chamber around them vibrated loudly. It was hard to stay on her feet with the floor constantly quaking beneath them. It was like they were standing on some invisible rocket that was about to launch and lift off.

There was an open hole in the wall nearby. Purdue kept his hands firmly placed on Julian to keep him at bay but all he could do was stare out that hole, out at the image of an icy, barren landscape. He was still surprised that he and Sam made across that horrible terrain. He had fully expected to be either shot by the Black Sun or would have just frozen before he ever reached the temple. Hypothermia would have been a terrible way to go.

The temple kept shaking but Purdue ignored

how off-balance it should have been making him. He kept focusing only on that small hole in the wall and the image that it made. Every bone in his body was rattling from the temple but he wouldn't look away from that hole. He wanted to see it. He wanted to.

There was a loud bang, like a boulder dropping down onto the ground.

Purdue blinked and suddenly, the hole in the wall showed a very different portrait. The white canvas of ice and snow was nowhere to be found. It was lush and green, an enormous field of grass that stretched out to the horizon. A sprawling meadow that gave off a much brighter feeling than that numb indifference of the Arctic.

The tremors subsided and Purdue just kept staring at that hole in the wall.

"We moved..." Sam whispered beside him. He wasn't looking at the wall. He was just staring at the chamber floors. He could just tell based on how the temple was reacting. "We must have."

"Aye," Purdue said beside him, still admiring the greenery of the new place he could see. "We most definitely did."

At least they had very obviously ended up in a much more comfortable climate than the Arctic had to offer. The challenge wasn't going to be the weather this time. It was going to be figuring out where the hell they ended up, and it was impossible to determine when they would move again. The temple had been planted firmly in isolation in the Arctic for quite some time, long enough to rob Lucius of his sanity. They might be trapped in the middle of nowhere for a long, long time. They were completely at the mercy of the Mayan temple and it's strange moving schedule.

"What a waste," Julian muttered from beside them, still trapped in Purdue and Sam's holds. He was also looking at the hole, straight out to the foreign landscape outside. He didn't looked impressed or happy about the change in scenery. Instead, he looked irritated. "All of those helicopters that we brought...and no one left to fly them. I hope you all enjoy rolling green hills and empty fields. Or how about this...you let me get my wish and I'll wish for all of us to be back home, safe and sound."

"Right," Sam snickered. "Because you're entirely trustworthy."

Julian was giggling to himself. "It is a wonder, though, isn't it? Why does this temple never like to stay in one place and how is it even moving so far, so quickly? Perhaps there are a thousand wheels tucked underneath it? Or it is sitting on top of a black hole. Questions to ponder..."

Nina couldn't listen to anymore of Julian's ramblings. Now that he was defeated, he seemed hell bent to just drive them all crazy with annoyance. Nina stormed out of the chamber but called back to her friends before she disappeared from sight. "I'm going to go help Elijah. Please let me know when we figure out what to do with him."

"Go," Purdue said to Sam. "I've got Julian right now."

"Are you sure?" Sam asked with some surprise. "What if he breaks free?"

"He won't," Purdue said with a wink. "But if he does, we won't let him get far. Go make sure all of the Black Sun operatives are out of this place. I'm sure it won't be sticking around the Arctic for very long."

Sam very obviously didn't want to go but finally let go after making sure Purdue had a good hold of Julian. He got up and followed after Nina. Purdue knocked Julian onto his stomach, keeping his arms locked behind his back, making sure that he was pinned down well enough to not have a hope of getting away.

"Aw, so this is your plan...send your friends away so you can do the deed yourself. That's awfully selfish of you, Mr. Purdue."

"Shut your mouth," Purdue said. "I'm sick of hearing you talk. Especially when you have no idea what you're talking about. You had your chance and you didn't get what you wanted. After everything you've done, it's time to answer for it all."

"And you're going to make me do that? Without the spear?"

"Aye."

Julian tried to writhe away from him, probably hoping that it would be easier now that it was only one man pinning him to the floor but Purdue had a strong hold of him that wasn't going to break very easily.

Purdue glanced to the left and saw Galen creeping up into the chamber. He didn't know where he'd been or how much of this struggle he had seen but Galen appeared with just as little gravitas as Purdue expected. Galen was a rat, and only waited until quiet moments to make any real moves. So there he stood, standing over the Spear of Destiny on the floor. The two of them locked eyes but Galen didn't stop his approach. Julian had apparently noticed Galen too, and immediately started barking orders.

"Get him!" He shouted from where he lay. "Kill him now! Now!"

Galen's gaze drifted to his boss but only for a couple of seconds before returning to Purdue. Without averting his eyes, he leaned down and picked up the spear, flashing that obnoxiously cheeky smile.

"I'll just be taking this," Galen said with an awkward laugh. He looked back to where Julian was pinned on the floor. "No hard feelings, eh? The spear should have been mine from the start, remember? And, if we're all being truthful sods here, I have always thought that you were shit."

Julian snarled at him venomously but couldn't do anything with Purdue on top of him. Galen looked over at Purdue and the smile on his face stretched out even further.

"See you around, Davy."

Galen turned and started making for the doorway. He hurried as quickly as he could with his crippled leg.

"You're just going to let that Irishman leave!?" Julian hissed.

"If it means keeping you here, aye. Absolutely." Purdue watched Galen disappear into the dark corridor outside, using the Spear of Destiny in conjunction with his cane to hasten his escape. "He can run pretty fast for a man with a bad leg. Still, it must be hard for you to see that no one is actually loyal to you at all."

Julian sneered. "They're nothing but sycophants anyway. Bootlickers and asskickers who aren't even fit to be part of the Order of the Black Sun. I should have purged the whole order when I took charge!"

"Aye, hindsight can be a real bastard. Like how I should have never let you come anywhere near the things that I care about."

"It doesn't matter," Julian said grinding his teeth like they were fangs. "You can win as many of these little fights as you want, Mr. Purdue. It does not make any difference in the end. I can't be stopped."

"I don't know about that," Purdue said. "You seem pretty stopped to me."

"I can't be killed!" Julian spat. "Especially now that you let someone run off with the one weapon that could actually harm me!"

"Perhaps not...but I didn't want to kill you anyway. Death isn't the only option."

Julian writhed and swiped at him like a

wounded animal. He was a far cry from the calm and collected terror that Purdue had met in that castle on the island of Rhodes. There was always the beast underneath his fine clothing but he so rarely let it slip out. Now, he might as well have been naked and seen for what he really was, a feral, murderous, monster that wasn't nearly as all-powerful as he pretended to be.

Julian's gray eyes were bloodshot with fury but Purdue was sick of looking at them.

He threw a hard punch down at his foe and knocked Julian Corvus out cold, closing those shards of ice in eye sockets and stopping his futile attempts to break free. For the first time since knowing Julian, the leader of the Black Sun was completely at Purdue's mercy now—and Purdue was long past the point of ever being merciful toward him. He knew exactly what he was going to do with the immortal demon that had been plaguing his life.

Sometimes, demons had to be locked away in boxes.

16

CHAPTER SIXTEEN – IN AN UNKNOWN LAND

Purdue, Nina, Elijah, Jean, and Sam stood outside of the Moving Temple of Ah Puch. They were surrounded by much nicer weather than they had up north. They tried to enjoy it, but it was hard to appreciate the weather when Charles' body was laying nearby. They weren't going to leave it in that temple, to be carted all over the world every so often until he was nothing but bones. As great of a housekeeper as he was, Purdue didn't want Charles' spirit to be stuck in that wretched place. That wouldn't have been fair.

"Where the hell are we?" Purdue asked, looking around. "Not that I'm complaining but...would we be able to hitch a ride home or what?"

Elijah pulled out his phone. A large crack ran along the center of it and Elijah swore under his breath. "That's perfect."

"You need to take better care of it," Nina said

with a weak smile. "You have been getting into too many fist fights. Probably busted it during all of your scuffles."

Elijah shook his head and tested it out with a swipe of his index finger. At least it still worked, and at least it was his phone rather than his glasses. He punched in a few directions into his GPS and then smirked.

"You won't believe it."

"We're in America aren't we?" Purdue groaned and crouched down with his face in his hands. "Goddamn that's some shit. The States don't deserve some place this nice."

"What's wrong with America?" Jean said with some offense.

"What's not wrong with America?" Purdue countered. "Well go on, where the hell are we?"

"The highlands."

Purdue shot to his feet. "What!? Like the highlands of Scotland? My highlands?"

Nina couldn't stop smiling. Sure enough, the more she looked at the green hills all around them, the more clear it became that she was looking at a Scottish glen. They were in the very middle of a valley tucked between the hills of the highlands.

Purdue turned around to face the temple and shouted at it. "Are you still granting wishes!? You sly bastard!"

"It's not..." Nina said, running her hands through her hair uncomfortably. "And it won't be ever again."

"And why's that?" Elijah asked.

"I broke the alta," Nina said, looking uncertain. "I wanted to make sure that no one tried to use it again. Or killed themselves and did use it. I just didn't...I just didn't want anything like this to happen again."

They all stood in silence as a breeze rolled past. No one really knew what to say and some were even feeling some mixed emotions about the whole thing. That kind of power was a hard thing to pass up, but they knew she was right. If that temple could make someone a god...it was too much. They'd seen firsthand that its power had unlimited reach. It conjured a novel and a drink for its sacrifice with ease. It could change the universe if used in the wrong hands—and it almost had been.

"I'm sorry," Nina said after a long moment. "I had to."

Purdue wrapped her arms around her and pulled her into a hug. Sam joined in and the three of them stood embracing for a long time. Elijah and Jean stood awkwardly a few feet away, neither a real part of that group but neither looked too upset by that. Neither of them were the kinds of people that enjoyed hugging it out for minutes at a time.

"I'm so glad you're alive," Purdue said. "There's so much I need to tell you."

"Same," Nina said with tears in her eyes. "It's been a hard few months."

"The hardest," Purdue agreed. "The very worst, aye."

"What do we do with him?" Jean interrupted, pointing at Julian who was still unconscious and tied up in the grass. "We could just leave him here."

"And let some tour group find him and set him free?" Purdue balked. "I don't think so. No I have my own plans for him. Once we get a car...and then a plane...do you mind showing me where the Order of the Black Sun call home?"

Nina and Elijah looked at one another, both stunned by the question. Neither must have been expecting to go back there anytime soon yet here they were, being asked to go straight back to the place that had functioned as their prison for so long.

"Why?"

"Like I said," Purdue said with a smirk. "I have plans."

They all started their walk across the highlands with the late great butler, Charles, being carried between Purdue and Sam while the captive former leader of the Black Sun was being dragged behind Elijah and Jean. Once they were at the top of the hill and ready to go down, they all looked back at the Moving Temple of Ah Puch. It was one of the strangest places they had ever been. There were times—like being dropped off in an almost perfect place—that it felt like there was some sort of life in that structure. Like all of the sacrifices that had been killed inside, all of the blood that had seeped into those cracks in the rocks, had given the temple its own blood and its own life. It almost felt alive—as alive as a temple could at least.

They all got one last look at it, knowing that it wouldn't be sitting there for very long. Maybe someday they would see that temple again, somewhere, on the far side of the world.

GALEN FITZGERALD'S time with the Order of the Black Sun had started off with so much promise. Right off the bat, he'd participated in the defeat of Purdue and from there, he went on so many successful assignments. He may not have been very popular with others within the secret society but he didn't care about that. He knew that if he slowly worked his way up, wormed his way into the right people's good graces, that someday they would have no choice but to give him their respect and admiration. Now that day would never come.

He knew a sinking ship when he saw one, and the Order of the Black Sun as moments away from being completely submerged. Their not-so-secret society was finished. Despite how it had looked at the start, Galen had chosen the losing team.

They were no longer in the frozen wasteland that they had entered the temple through. All of the helicopters that the order had brought were gone. Now they were surrounded by an enormous series of meadows, a lush green sea with rolling emerald hills. It made things more difficult than

Galen had planned on. It would have been easy to just hop into a chopper and fly the hell out. Now they had to walk until they found new civilization —but at least they weren't going to be freezing.

Soon enough, that temple would hop somewhere else.

"Well...this all turned into a nice big storm of shit, eh?" Galen said, turning to Oniel beside him. The mute nodded, still glaring back at the temple. He obviously still wanted his vengeance. Galen couldn't fault him for that; he was craving the same thing but today was very clearly not the right day to make that happen.

Galen held his cane in one hand and the Spear of Destiny in the other. His fingers squeezed them both tightly in his grasp.

"Davy has to ruin everything...that bastard."

At least they had gotten away before being dragged down with the rest of the Black Sun. This was really all Julian Corvus's fault. That loon wouldn't listen to him and had failed to kill Purdue, despite all of his wasted efforts. That was with the Black Sun's arsenal of ancient artifacts and superior numbers, as well as Julian's apparent immortality. He'd still lost. He deserved to go down for all of his failures as their leader—but Galen refused to be dragged down with that psychopath.

Galen always prided himself on being a survivor, and he had gotten away from all of his progress collapsing around him. Getting the hell out was the only option. They could deal with Davy another day. This was just another thing to add to the long list of grievances Galen had with David Purdue.

He examined the Spear of Destiny—the artifact that had reunited him with David Purdue in the first place. The search for that spear is what had brought him into contact with the Order of the Black Sun to begin with. So much had happened since then. Part of him wished he had never called Purdue to ask for help finding the spear. Things could have—and would have—gone so differently.

At least he ended up with the spear. It was a small victory but he would gladly take what he could get at this point. Even a small victory was far better than the defeat that the rest of the Black Sun was suffering. Purdue might have beaten all of them, but Galen hadn't let Davy beat him too.

Galen looked back at the Mayan temple. They moved further and further away and the temple faded into the distance. Purdue was back there, probably celebrating and feeling so superior to everyone else.

Davy was probably so happy—but Galen wouldn't let him feel that way for long.

17

CHAPTER SEVENTEEN – THE BOOKS

After making their way back to a small Scottish town, Purdue had managed to get them a car for free. There were quite a few people in Scotland that were willing to help him or felt obligated to help when Purdue cashed in old favors. From there, they were able to get to the airport where Purdue chartered another private plane. Following Elijah's instructions, they made their to the Order of the Black Sun's home base.

Purdue wasn't impressed with what he saw. He expected more from such a prestigious secret society. It was actually somewhat of a dump. A hidden base in the middle of nowhere.

"So what now?"

Sam straightened his posture. "I say we pack up all of the artifacts that they took and then we burn this whole place to the ground, just like they did to your house. We wipe the Order of the Black Sun off the face of the Earth for good."

Purdue shook his head. "If you ask me, that would be a truly terrible waste."

Both of his colleagues' mouths practically dropped to their feet. Nina and Sam exchanged concerned glances and then just kept gawking at Purdue. They were definitely not expecting to say anything like that. This was their chance to finally eradicate the Black Sun for good but Purdue had given it a lot of thought, despite what everyone thought he would naturally want.

"What the hell are you talking about?" Sam's cheeks were red. "We can finally end this! We won. The Black Sun lost."

Purdue understood Sam's reasoning, but he still gave another firm shake of his skull. "Beating Julian...burning their headquarters down...taking all of the artifacts away from here...it won't get rid of all of the Black Sun members. If we scatter all of these megalomaniacs to the wind, do you really think it ends here? You think no one will try and take charge? That they won't reform and come after us again? Hell, I bet that is what that bastard Galen is up to already."

The risk was too great. All they had done was cut the head off of the snake, but the rest of its body was still very dangerous and in this situation, capable of growing an entirely new head. And the next one might even be more venomous than the last.

"It may be better to keep the order together as

best as we can. We can steer the Black Sun into a more...positive...direction."

Sam looked utterly bewildered by what he was hearing and all of Purdue's reasoning apparently washed over him without even crossing his mind. "So we just ignore everything that happened? Let bygones be bygones? The Order of the Black Sun tried to kill us so many times!"

"And they won't ever again," Purdue said firmly. "Not if we're the ones calling the shots from now on. They had bad leadership—really, really bad—but the Black Sun has resources that we don't have on our own. We could use the Black Sun as a tool to help us."

"This is ridiculous," Sam said, crossing his arms.

"Is it?" Purdue let out a little laugh. Sometimes Sam could be so hardheaded. "Seems sensible enough to me. Honestly, I think you're still a bit sour that the Black Sun girl fooled you with a pretty face, aye?"

"That's not it!" Sam snapped, but wasn't very convincing.

"Of course it's not," Purdue teased with a wink. "You want the Black Sun out of our hair, then this is the best way to neutralize them for good. Otherwise, we're just putting out one fire and waiting for another to come along."

Nina had stood by and listened to the debate but neither of the two men were budging on their positions. She was watching two little boys fight over something petty when they should all be on the same page. She got between them, ready to knock their heads together.

"If anyone should be making this decision, it should be me. I was the Black Sun's prisoner for a long time. Sure, they tried to kill you. Sure, they took your things. They didn't lock you in a small little box for months! I want to get rid of this whole group just as much as you."

Sam looked pleased, finally getting some support.

"But Purdue is right."

Sam's expression fell immediately.

"The only way to really beat them is to take control of them. And their resources could be absolutely invaluable to us. You should see their deep vaults. They've got everything you can think of in there."

"I don't believe this," Sam groaned. "So if we can't beat them...join them? That old chestnut?"

"No," Purdue said. "We beat them, and we're not joining them. We're redefining the teams altogether."

"CHARLES DIDN'T DESERVE to go out so bloody."

That was the undeniable truth and it was all Purdue could think as he looked at Charles. He was lying so still, but his chest was still stained with dry blood from the wound that had killed him. In those last moments, he had looked so afraid. During his time in captivity, he must have felt at least a little comfort after gaining immortality from the Spear of Destiny. He hadn't attained it by choice but once he had it, he must have felt at least a little happy that death wouldn't be able to touch him. But it had, and now he was gone for good.

Purdue thought about all of the times he had been there for him. Whether it was helping him prepare for his many exploits or just helping him move around the artifacts in the collection room. All of those delicious dinners that Charles had prepared, the rides he had given him that were always filled with such wise words of advice during hard times. He had always been there to support him. By the end of it all, he was the closest family he had.

Most butlers would have advised against the majority of things David Purdue took part in. Most would have never, ever gone along with any of his plans or his ideas for success. They would have tucked tail and run, thinking that Purdue was nothing more than a billionaire thrill seeker who was willing to throw his life away for some excitement. They never would have understood why he really did what he did.

Charles understood him, he always had.

There was no one more reliable in the world than that butler.

It hurt to think that he would still be alive if Purdue had just been a little bit more normal; if he had less dangerous hobbies, then Charles would have spent a quiet life serving dishes, cleaning up after some spoiled rich brat, and taking leisurely drives around the countryside. Instead, he served a house that had been invaded and destroyed by a secret society.

There were probably very few butlers in the world that had been taken hostage by murderers and been stabbed by a holy weapon like the Spear of Destiny. He was an oddity among his peers, but that was part of why he was gone.

Purdue couldn't help but think about what Charles might have been thinking at the end. Did he regret helping Purdue? Did he regret supporting all of his globetrotting adventures or obsession with collecting some of history's most interesting relics? Did he regret it all? He hoped not.

"He was a good man," Sam said with a nod. "Always was. He was wonderful to talk to anytime I was over the house. And he could prepare a hell of a meal. And if it wasn't for Charles, you never would have been able to maintain that place. It would have burned down a lot sooner than it actually did, wouldn't it?"

Purdue managed a laugh. "That's true."

"You should have seen him when we were prisoners," Nina interjected. "He gave them hell for what they did to you. When we all thought you were dead...he wasn't giving them an inch. Wanted to kill all of them for hurting you. Through the failed escape attempt and even when he was killed and revived by the Julian to test the Spear of Destiny, he never broke down and never gave up. He was resilient to the very end."

As terrible of an image it was to think of Charles rotting in some dungeon, it was comforting to know that it never beat him down and that he persevered through it all. Despite his advanced age, that old man was tough as hell. No one could take that away from him, even now.

And in the end, he did help triumph over the Order of the Black Sun.

Purdue absolutely felt guilty about his role leading up to Charles dying but he also took comfort that it seemed Charles wouldn't have wanted it any other way.

He couldn't stop thinking about the moment when bullets were racing toward him and Charles had stood in the way. He blocked the bullets' path with his own body. He may have been immortal at the time and able to withstand them, but Purdue knew the truth—that Charles would have put himself between his boss and those bullets no matter what, with or without the immortality.

Charles was more than his butler. He was his friend.

He always had been.

They covered his body, but made sure to keep Twenty Thousand Leagues Under the Sea beside him. His last wish on that altar as he died was to conjure that book out of thin air. It was a simple wish and a far cry from Julian's hopes of godhood and world domination, but it was no less important. They would honor his final wish.

Purdue thought back to a night when Charles was sitting in one of the lounge chairs by the fireplace. He had built the fire himself and was sitting beside it with so much pride, knowing that his hard work had brought him immeasurable relaxation. He had Twenty Thousand Leagues Under the Sea by his side like he usually did during his rest times.

"It's always that one," Purdue had said. "I feel like you've been reading it for years. What's taking so long? Slow read?"

Charles just gave a knowing smile. "I would give anything to be able to read this novel for the first time again, but alas, my first reading of it was long ago when I was a very, very young man. No, I have loved this book for decades, sir. I have read it hundreds of times."

"Hundreds, aye?" Purdue stood over him, his arms folded, bewildered by what he was hearing. "The same story hundreds of times. You know all the characters. You know all the plot twists. You know how it ends. Hell, you must know every single word on every single page by heart by now. Don't you ever get bored?"

"Bored?" Charles looked stunned by the question, like he couldn't fathom why it would ever be asked. "Heavens no, sir! How could I ever be bored by such a perfect story. The exploits of the Nautilus, led by the steadfast Captain Nemo! Going out of his way to explore places that the world had never seen. Facing challenges that most men could never comprehend. Persevering through it all despite all of the odds being stacked against him. Adventure. Discovery. It has it all."

It just occurred to Purdue—looking at his butler's lifeless body resting beside that book that he loved so much—that Charles' favorite novel might have been exactly why he had so diligently helped Purdue for so long. He didn't just want to read about the exploits of one man traveling the world and discovering amazing things, he wanted to be part of it. He wanted to help make that story he loved become a reality, and David Purdue was just as much of an adventurer as Captain Nemo.

Without Charles, those exploits he went on would be far different. There wouldn't be a warm meal and a smooth drink waiting for him upon his return from his travels. There wouldn't be someone he could count on to make the preparations for his expeditions.

Nina took Purdue's hand and squeezed it tight.

"He loved you like a son, you know."

Purdue smiled and picked up the Jules Verne novel. Charles wouldn't have wanted him to just throw it away or bury it with him. He would want Purdue to read it and take in every single page of it. And that was exactly what Purdue intended to do.

"Aye, I know he did."

THERE WAS another book besides Twenty Thousand Leagues Under the Sea that was on Purdue's mind, but he hadn't given it much thought since Jean-Luc had used it to help hurt Julian. It was only when Jean looked like he was ready to depart, that that book of shadows found its way back to the forefront of Purdue's thoughts.

Jean gave them all a curt nod. “It's been...a crazy few months...but I'll be on my way then. Hopefully, they haven't cleared out my shop.”

Purdue didn't miss the dark leather-bound book tucked under Jean-Luc's arm. He gave a cough and then nodded toward the journal.

“And where do you think you're taking that book?”

Jean faked some surprise, acting as if he didn't realize he still had the book of shadows but Purdue saw right through that faux embarrassment.

Purdue continued, shaking his head. “I seem to recall that we found that spell book together, and we determined that it would be the safest in my care, aye? Isn't that right?”

Jean gave a little laugh, but it just barely slipped through the tension that was starting to form on his face. He was getting defensive.

“We did decide that it would be safest with you, yes...but how well did that turn out?”

Purdue couldn't exactly argue with that point. Almost immediately after they had put the pages of the book of shadows together, all of Purdue's artifacts were taken and then all hell broke loose.

The book of shadows was the only thing he had been able to hold onto at that time. The one thing he could salvage from that horrible defeat.

"I kept it out of the Black Sun's hands at least," Purdue said.

"But if was far too close of a call for my comfort. Looking for this book is what began our partnership...I have just as much claim to it as you do. More even...since I have proven that I understand how to use its contents."

He wasn't wrong about that either. Jean-Luc Gerard was an expert in the occult studies and his years of accumulating that knowledge had allowed him to use far more of the book's power than Purdue ever could. Hell, Purdue was so intimidated by the pages inside that he barely ever opened the book at all. When it came to a supernatural—one might even say haunted—relic like that grimoire, he was a novice. Maybe he wasn't the best person to be the book's keeper after all.

Jean could clearly see the wheels turning in Purdue's head. He smiled, knowingly. "You know I'm right."

"I do," Purdue admitted. "It's just...we went through a lot to get that book, remember? It's tough to part ways with something that you worked so hard to get."

"I understand and I agree," Jean said, having been with him every step of that way of that particular journey. "We went through a lot to get that book but you have your collection of all kinds of artifacts back, and the items in the Black Sun's vaults too. You have more than enough old trinkets to keep you company."

Purdue did feel a little selfish, but he wasn't used to having to give away his things. He much preferred hording them and keeping them safe. But after Julian Corvus and the Order of the Black Sun raided his collection, his faith in himself was rattled. He wasn't as confident that he could protect his own belongings anymore. And now that he had all of those relics back, he wanted to hold onto them more tightly than ever.

But when it came down to it, Jean was right. He was a better choice to keep the book of shadows safe.

Jean gave a toothy smile. "If you're really that heartbroken about losing it, you're always welcome to come on down to the store and take a peek at it...with my permission of course."

Purdue smiled back. "Fair enough."

Jean's face flushed with surprise. "Really?"

"Really. I trust you, Jean. Just think of it as a reward for the months of shit you went through with the Black Sun."

"Wow," Jean said, looking at the old book in his hands. "I thought I was going to have to pry the book out of your cold, dead hands."

Purdue put his hands up in surrender and chuckled. "There's no need for anything like that. It's yours."

Jean's fingers tightened on the book in his

hands, squeezing it tight, like he was afraid it was going to blow away. It was no secret how long he had been hoping to read the completed book of shadows. He had started off with only one page, and now here he was, finally in possession of the book, with no one setting any parameters or restrictions. He could finally read it and study its power to his heart's content.

Jean looked up, his eyes wide but full of appreciation. "Thank you."

"You're welcome," Purdue said with a causal shrug, trying to make it seem like it wasn't a big deal at all. "Honestly, that journal gives me all kinds of bad feelings. My life will be a lot nicer without it being around to creep me out. That witch, Mona Greer, has been haunting me far too long...but I'm sure I'll be in New Orleans at some point, so you owe me a whole fun day on Bourbon Street."

"Drinks are on me," Jean said, holding the book up. "Or maybe I could just conjure us up as many drinks as we want. Who knows?"

"Happy reading," Purdue said. "And safe travels home. I'll see you around at some point."

When Jean-Luc Gerard was gone, Purdue realized that some of his more recent acquisitions were finding their way into others' hands. Galen took the Spear of Destiny and now Jean-Luc could finally add the book of shadows to his little bookshop's shelves. The people who had been part of those respective ventures were winding up with those artifacts in the end—for better or worse.

But if Purdue had his way, then Galen wouldn't have the Spear of Destiny for long. That would need to be addressed. The less threats that he had from now on, the better things would be. The things Purdue had in mind for the future would be hard enough without having to worry about grudges that should have been buried a long time ago.

WHEN THE NEWS stations dared to go back to the Mayan temple in the Arctic, there was very little for them to find. The temple was nowhere to be found and left no trace that it had ever been there at all. The only things that remained were the circle of black helicopters that once formed a perimeter around the place. The other was the body of a young woman, who coroners later determined had died from a large fall. They would never discover the handful of guards that were dead under the ice a short distance away. No one could explain it but many of the reporters regretted listening to that mysterious organization that demanded that they leave for a short while. Whatever had happened, it had taken their big news story from them.

They had no idea how the temple bounced around different parts of the world. They had no idea that they should even still be looking for it anywhere. To them, it had just dissipated from all existence and the best they could do would be to wait and hope something similar happened again. If it ever did, they would have the attention of the entire world back in their hands.

With the discovery of a body at the scene, though, came investigative measures. Upon further research of the victim found on the ice, having fallen to her death from a building that no longer seemed to exist, they found no records of the young woman's identity. She had no matching fingerprints and wasn't identified by any facial recognition software. She might as well have been a ghost since there was no indication of who she was before her death.

The girl was nameless and completely unidentifiable. There was nothing about her that they could use to help figure out who she was. She was a perfectly blank slate, with nothing to leave behind but a few frozen tears. They would never figure out who she was, but that was rather fitting given Kendra's own views of herself. She would have told them that there was nothing to figure out, since the victim hadn't been anyone at all. She was simply the mannequin that would dress up sometimes, pretend to be someone else, but never have a soul of her own.

The reporters and investigators knew that there was a piece of the story that they were missing, but they didn't know how large of a chunk it really was. They would never know that they were standing on the remnants of a battlefield where a feud between one former billionaire and a secret society took place. That was the story that they would really want, but they had less of evidence of it existing than they did of that young victim's identity.

There was nothing left behind in the Arctic, not really. Nothing but an unknown dead woman, a handful of stolen helicopters, and a missing Mayan temple. It wasn't even worth publishing a follow up story. Most people already probably thought it was a hoax.

They would never know the truth of what happened inside that temple.

18

CHAPTER EIGHTEEN – RESTRUCTURING

The facility was nearly empty. Most members of the Black Sun had scattered to the ends of the earth, slunk into the holes that they had initially crawled out of, abandoned the cause the second they lost. Elijah felt proud to have been part of that defeat and he walked through the empty facility with a great deal of satisfaction. For so long, those halls had been filled with arrogant murderers that thought they could just steamroll their way through the rest of the world. There were a few that remained, mostly the new recruits who weren't entirely sure what had even happened or whose side they were supposed to be on.

The Order of the Black Sun had so recently been reorganized under the leadership of Julian Corvus. That psychopath had meticulously restructured how things operated within the order. He got rid of the old leadership like the council and the veterans that couldn't and wouldn't adapt to his new ways. He had recruited ambitious minds with useful skill sets that he could mold and twist for the future plans he had. He had made an already dangerous organization downright vicious in how they performed their objectives. There was no code of conduct and there was no rule except one—to serve the Order of the Black Sun without question.

But now, that new order he had forged had shattered completely into millions of pieces; from the lowest informants, spies, and consultants, to the brutal enforcers and agents strong-arming their way to priceless pieces of history all over the globe. Even the inner most circle of the order had seen their best laid plans fall apart before their eyes.

Julian Corvus promised them all a new age where the Order of the Black Sun would shine on the entire world, and they would have a chance to truly make a difference, not just to themselves but to everyone. And at first, he really did seem to be leading them in a new and bold direction. Those promises seemed like they were actually going to be kept, but in the end, he wasn't the right person to follow. His psychopathic tendencies weren't what the order needed. They didn't need the cruelty. They didn't need the malice. They didn't need the delusions of grandeur. The Black Sun didn't really need anything Julian was promising them.

After all of his empty promises and passionate assurances, Julian Corvus hadn't made the Black Sun any better.

"I am the change."

That is what he had said; that was his declaration. It wasn't true at all and was only another lie to help him seize power uncontested. He told them all what they wanted to hear and so many soaked it in because it was what they wanted so badly. The ones who didn't believe him mostly stayed quiet out of fear of what would happen if they spoke out. It wouldn't have been anything good and they all knew that.

Now it was clear enough that the Order of the Black Sun had never truly changed. If there was any change, it hadn't been for the better. If anything, they were far worse off now than they had been under the old leaders.

Even after all of the internal strife and the drastic changes that were made, the Black Sun still couldn't even defeat David Purdue. That single man had held up a mirror and showed them how fruitless all of their efforts had been and that they were only pretending to have improved. The Black Sun didn't shine any brighter than before.

And now in the fallout of Julian's reign, the Black Sun was in ruins. Most of their top members weren't going to be continuing their membership, one way or another. Some had been forced out, were in the process of being forced out, while others scattered to the wind, trying to abandon the sinking ship they were on.

People that had once devoted their lives to the order were long gone.

Sasha was one of their best enforcers for a time but even she had seen that Julian was leading the order to destruction. Her attempts to turn the tables on him through helping Purdue ended with her dead under a pile of rubble. She could have maybe been a suitable replacement as leader one day just as Elijah knew she wished for, but they would never know now. Elijah sometimes wished he had understood Sasha's concerns earlier. He might have even tried to help conspire against Julian's new brand of leadership. But, unfortunately, Sasha had seen the truth too early, before anyone else was willing to see it too. It was a shame that someone who wanted to push the Order of the Black Sun into a more civilized direction was killed before this battle. She probably would have loved to have seen Julian finally brought down.

Galen Fitzgerald was another case altogether. He had done surprisingly well for himself within the order, all things considered. Despite annoying just about everyone he had spoken to, he had made allies and completed many retrieval operations. He was seen as a joke by most but had proven that there was occasionally something backing up all of his narcissistic posturing. He was petty and materialistic, but everyone had to admit he was quite the survivor—like a slippery cockroach. He had survived the decimation of the order and had remained relatively unscathed. He had come out of it in better condition than most of the other operatives. Escaping with the Spear of Destiny wasn't a bad consolation prize either, and had apparently cut ties with the Black Sun for good. That was fine by Elijah. That Irishmen had plenty of hot air in his body to find his own path.

He would probably be writing his next self-righteous autobiography soon. Elijah could think of a few fitting titles just off the top of his head. *Wounded Leg: How I Made the Most of My Time in a Secret Society*. Or maybe, *I'm a Survivor: The True Tale Of How I Survived Through Experiences That Should Have Killed Me*. Then again, there was always, *How Not to Be Liked By My Coworkers*. That one would be very insightful considering how much experience he had in that department.

Whatever title Galen went with, the book was sure to be just as nauseating as his first, nothing more than a self-aggrandizing story about why he was so great. At least the sequel would have more interesting material to work with, though Galen would probably waste that and only focus on his parts. It would be a real shame if Elijah was cut from the story, but he would understand. He hadn't spent much time with Galen because the man was an insufferable gnat.

Then, of course, there was Julian Corvus himself. The Order of the Black Sun had crumbled and that fall started from the very top. He had gone from being a feared but effective grunt to having complete control over the rest of the order. It was practically a Cinderella story that could inspire so many prospective recruits but unfortunately, his ascension was a violent one. The ladder he climbed was stained with the blood of all of the people he had butchered on his way to the top. He was a tyrant—and his rule had been mercifully short.

If anyone was to blame for this defeat, it was him. This was all part of his great big master plan. He had taken over the Black Sun with a mix of force and charisma and could have taken the order into any direction that he wanted. He could have been smart and led them to greatness but instead they followed him straight down into failure.

Julian might have been more effective if he hadn't allowed his sadism to take over all of his decisions. His plans became reliant on how much they made Purdue suffer. Making decisions like that might have been fine during times like attacking Purdue's home but otherwise, a mindset like that was nothing more than a distraction. His psychotic urges to relish others' pain made him a very unstable leader—and instability made it much easier for things to collapse under everyone.

And it had—the Order of the Black Sun might finally be finished for good and Elijah really didn't mind as long as all of those relics in the deep vault were kept safe. Maybe Purdue would take all of them, a victor claiming his spoils of war. Only time would tell how everything would shake out in the end. It was just nice knowing that many of the world's most dangerous people might no longer have a clubhouse to play in anymore.

Elijah hoped that the black sun would finally set for good.

If not, then he hoped it would be a little less dark.

PURDUE HADN'T SEEN his trophies in a long time—far too long.

His private collection had always meant so much to him. It was a trove of reminders of all of the many experiences he had gone through, the adventures he had been a part of. They were all extremely valuable to the rest of the world, but they had an extra bit of sentimental value for him. So many of them weren't even supposed to exist, yet Purdue had touched them, taken them, and protected them in his collection.

Unfortunately, he hadn't been able to protect them forever. The time he spent without them was hard enough, but there was an extra sting knowing that all of those priceless relics of history—both known and lost—had been taken away under his watch. They had fallen into the wrong hands because he'd underestimated his enemies, and all of those pieces of history had been put at risk.

At least things seemed to have turned out alright. He even had the Order of the Black Sun's own collection now in his hands. So many relics that they had misused or wielded to enact their dangerous objectives, but Purdue wouldn't let those relics ever be used in that way ever again. Now there was an even larger responsibility to protect his relics, since he had more than twice as many as before.

Purdue looked down into the deep vault, a cylindrical hole in the floor where most of the artifacts were stored. A large crane hung over it, which could be guided by computer to pull out or put in the proper containers storing the items. It was a bit sad to see all of those relics put away in such a way, where they were buried and hidden from the world until the Black Sun had any use for them. At least when he used to hold onto them, he put them on display, so he could at least think about the items that had centuries, and sometimes millennia of historical significance.

Then again, that might have been one of the reasons he lost them. If he put everything in a hole like the Black Sun did, then they would probably be harder to steal. So they had that going for them at least, as much as it seemed disrespectful.

"Impressive, right?" Nina said, walking toward him.

He whistled as he looked down into the hole. "That's one word for it. It certainly seems secure."

"It is," Nina said. "I spent a fair amount of time in here during my time as a prisoner. They had me helping Elijah Dane curate all of the relics that they brought in before storing them away."

"That doesn't sound so bad," Purdue said with a wink.

"It wasn't...but it didn't last long..."

"What happened?"

"I tried to escape, obviously," Nina said with some shame. "Almost made it out too but Elijah turned us in when we tried."

"The same Elijah that you're now sort of friends with?" Purdue was a little confused by it all, but he was sure it made much more sense if he had been imprisoned with her.

"Yeah, him," Nina said with an awkward laugh. "Elijah ended up really helping us escape later. It took some convincing but he was a prisoner of the Black Sun's for far longer than we were. He ended up working for them just so he didn't have to rot in a cell like we did."

"I see," Purdue said, softening on Elijah a little. He was still a bit suspicious of anyone who had a such an intimate relationship with the order but Nina kept assuring him that he was on their side. Hopefully she was right.

There were footsteps from near the large open doors that led into the vault room. Elijah Dane entered, looking quite anxious. Purdue studied him closely as he approached. He didn't seem quite as openly crazy as Julian, Kendra, Victor Moore, and all of the other newer Black Sun members that Purdue had encountered but for all he knew, he could just have been better at hiding it.

Elijah straightened his glasses, readying himself for whatever their decision was going to be. After all, he was part of the Black Sun; if the order was going down, then he would be dragged down with them. He just had to accept that fate. All of his choices had culminated toward this moment.

"You look nervous," Purdue said. "Cheer up, aye?"

"Apologies..." Elijah didn't even remotely perk up. "It's rather difficult to be cheerful when you've lost the best chance you had at fulfilling your life's work. Awful as Julian and the order was, it presented me with items that I never would have been able to examine elsewhere. Museums and exhibits are all well and good, but they don't have..." Elijah stretched out his arms, trying to encapsulate the whole room. "...they don't have this."

Purdue and Nina peered around.

"You're right," Purdue said. "But this place still does and with me in charge, it still will. And those artifacts will need a guardian now more than ever."

"What do you mean you in charge?" Elijah picked at his ear. Nothing he was hearing sounded right. "I am not sure that I follow..."

"From what Nina has told me, you respect the importance of all of these relics. You see their real worth, and she also told me what you did for her through all of that time she was a prisoner.

Elijah glanced at Nina uncertainly. Their time together had a lot of ups and downs. There had been slights and disagreements, betrayals even. Despite coming together at the end, did helping her escape absolve him all of all of the bad things he had let happen to her in those cells?

Purdue continued. "The Order of the Black Sun is going to be very different...but that doesn't mean that everything had to be. We will be taking control of this entire organization, and we will be purging all of the bad, aye...but why not keep the good?"

"So you're going to be the new boss...and you're what, offering me a job?"

"It's already your job," Purdue said with a laugh. "All I'm asking is if you will stay at your post."

Elijah looked baffled but his face swelled with relief and even some happiness. His usual robotic passiveness turned into a surprised smile.

"Absolutely."

19

CHAPTER NINETEEN - THE LATEST ADDITION TO THE COLLECTION

Julian woke up and slowly got to his feet. There were artifacts all around him. He recognized many of them as things that he had taken from David Purdue's estate, and others were part of the Order of the Black Sun's own collection.

Purdue stood a few feet away. His arms were crossed but he was smiling like he was the happiest man in the world. Seeing him look so pleased sent a wave of anger through Julian. He rushed forward, ready to wipe that stupid smirk off of Purdue's face but he didn't get very far at all. Julian collided with an invisible barrier—no, not invisible—he just hadn't noticed it right away. There was a slight glare around him and he realized he was surrounded by glass walls, and that glass had apparently been reinforced since it didn't come close to shattering on impact.

Julian pressed his palm against the glass. His

surprise was drowned out by his anger, but he couldn't help but feel a little impressed.

"What is this exactly, Mr. Purdue?" Julian ran the tips of his fingers along the inside of his glass cage. "What have you done?"

Purdue just clapped his hands together like he had just invented something incredible. With that same victorious glee, he finally spoke to his prisoner. "I've been all over the world. So many countries, so many places. I've seen so many strange things...things most people would never ever believe actually existed. Out of all of those things I've seen firsthand...everything that these eyes have been able to see...I have never seen something like you. A real oddity, a rarity. You're just as valuable as all of the other priceless relics I've collected. Maybe even more...so this seemed like the perfect place to put you. You wanted my collection so bad? Here it is. You're part of it now."

Julian sneered. "You can't do this."

"I already have," Purdue said with a shrug, and gestured to the cage to point out the obvious. "You didn't give me much of a choice, Julian. You were a threat to the whole world...and there weren't many options to stop you. How do you bring down a guy like you when killing is off the table, aye? There's no putting you down for good with a bullet like anyone else. That already makes you a real pain in the arse. And with all of those connections of yours, I doubt a prison would do much good. No...no, you needed to be somewhere that I could keep an eye on you, Mr. Immortal Man."

Julian shook his head and started wrapping his knuckles against the glass. He licked his lips, looking like a caged beast, trying to figure out how to break free from his constraints. "I...I seem to recall that you have trouble keeping a hold of your personal things. And you think that this place will hold me any better? You think you're going to keep me here?"

"I do," Purdue said. "This isn't just a panic room in my basement this time. If you have any friends out there that will try to set you free, they're going to have a far tougher time taking my things than you did. For all of the trouble you caused me, I did learn from that particular defeat. And this time...I have all of the many resources of the Order of the Black Sun at my disposal."

Julian's usual smug visage was peeling away. The demon beneath that facade was rearing its ugly head like it always did when he wasn't in control.

"No," Julian growled. "What are you babbling about? You don't have the Black Sun."

"I do, actually." All of your loyalists ran from that temple. They haven't shown themselves since. Even Galen went scurrying away like the rat bastard he is. No one is going to even try to rescue you or try to put you back on the throne. No one is going to try to reinstate you as the leader of the order."

Julian tapped the glass harder.

"It seems you should have picked better friends, aye? It turns out that there were quite a few in the Black Sun that didn't want to follow you but were afraid that you would do to them what you did to the old ruling council. From what I hear, you butchered them during a board meeting."

A demented flash of nostalgia crossed Julian's face but then slipped away, overtaken by his growing frustration with his current situation.

"Fear is an effective tool, I'll give you that one but it's useless once the threat has been removed. We both know you were never the right person to lead the Order of the Black Sun."

"But you are?" Julian cackled, his hand screeching across the glass. "You have done nothing but go against the order! You don't even want it!"

"You're right. Aye. I don't want it. I never have. If I had it my way, the Order of the Black Sun would be dismantled and buried forever. But someone needs to steer this shit secret society into the right direction...if it has to be me, then so be it. I'll do a hell of a lot better than you did. I can guarantee that much. It won't be hard at all."

Julian looked around and his gaze filled with recollection.

"Aye," Purdue said with a smirk. He'd been waiting for Julian to notice and realize just where he was. "You recognize it. Like I said, this isn't my basement this time. That cellar probably isn't even there anymore after what you did. This is so much better. You're in the Order of the Black Sun's vaults. Elijah Dane helped set this up. The way I see it...you took my home, so it's only fair that I take yours."

Julian's taps against the glass turned into violent smacks, trying desperately to smash through his cell. "I'll kill you for this."

Purdue raised his arms expectantly. "You're welcome to try but you haven't had the best luck so far and it will only be harder to do from in there."

"I'll get out," Julian hissed. "One way or another."

"Maybe eventually...but it won't be today. Thanks to the Spear of Destiny, you've got plenty of time to try. Immortality is brilliant and all...until you're stuck some place you don't want to be. Eternity can feel like a very, very long time. Hell...I'd say it is quite a long time, wouldn't you?"

Julian bored his teeth like a caged lion, now smashing his fists against the glass over and over. His strikes continued to have no effect on the glass box he was trapped in but he kept trying anyway, to no avail. Those icy gray eyes of his looked like they were melting from the furious fire behind them. He roared and kept punching the glass but it was futile, no matter how hard he hit it. His knuckles tore and grew bloody but the everlasting power in his body mended them second later. He could keep trying to centuries to come. Julian Corvus was truly trapped and now he was accepting it. That demon was finally stuck in a box, removed from the outside world.

Purdue watched his nemesis struggle for a few minutes. It was undeniably satisfying and even a little cathartic. When he turned, Julian's shouts of rage just grew louder. "You will die for this, Purdue! Do you hear me!? You will die for this! You will! The Order of the Black Sun will not stand for this!"

Purdue turned back but only enough to see Julian. "Don't worry. The Order of the Black Sun will be better than ever. Funny how things turn out, aye?"

When he left the Black Sun vaults, the enormous door closed behind Purdue. He heard its many locks seal with in it. No one would be getting in or out of there that wasn't supposed to. His latest acquisition was safe and sound inside, and wouldn't be disturbed—and it would never have the chance to disturb the rest of the world ever again.

Nina and Sam stood there waiting for him. Nina glanced at the vault door with some pride. "How is he doing in there?"

"Not great," Purdue said. "But I'm sure he'll get used to it...he'll have to."

"If it was anyone else, I might question it..." Sam said bluntly. "But that bastard deserves every second of it."

"Yes, he most certainly does," Nina said. "So what's next?"

Purdue had some ideas about that. "We use all

of this to actually help the world. This isn't about trophies or anything like that...as much as I love those. We could really make a difference here. The Order of the Black Sun could actually be a good thing now."

"I think we should change the name," Sam said. "Just saying...it leaves a bad taste in my mouth. It makes me feel like I'm about to be kidnapped, shot at, or just annoyed. All my paranoia starts nagging at me when we say it."

"We should keep it the same," Nina argued. "We shouldn't forget how horrible it was. The order has been a stain on history and everything we're trying to preserve. We shouldn't try and rewrite what happened. We should make it have a better place in history in the long run, redefine what this organization even is."

"Agreed," Purdue said. I love the idea that the Order of the Black Sun could help the world."

They walked out of the building and Purdue looked up at the bright blue sky. Fluffy clouds danced across it. It was a strikingly beautiful day, like the universe itself was congratulating them on their victory.

The yellow sun above them seemed brighter than it had in a long time.

20

CHAPTER TWENTY – THE BUTLER'S LAST WISH

Purdue hadn't been back to his old estate since the night it burned to the ground. He had nearly died in there, cooked alive inside. So much had happened since that night. He had wandered around with not a coin to his name, having to rummage for scraps in the street. He had to make deals with modern day pirates in search of centuries old gold, waiting for a mutiny to take place at any moment. He had dived to the deepest and darkest depths of the ocean, and had used the power of the ocean itself to help dodge torpedoes on his way back up to the surface. He had to overcome a cursed sword that he could never lose track of or risk dying from a sudden heart attack. All the while, Julian Corvus and the Order of the Black Sun was moving forward with their plans.

It felt so long ago, but at the same time, it felt like it had only been five minutes since he was last inside. He could still picture how it once was so vividly, each and every room in the enormous house. He remembered the wallpaper, the carpets, and the little decorations strewn about the entire mansion.

He had spent so much time in all of the rooms. He slept in the gigantic bed every night, and had eaten thousands of the meals prepared by Charles that were all perfectly placed on the dining room table.

As Purdue drove back toward his decimated home, he had Twenty Thousand Leagues Under the Sea in the passenger's seat. He was reminded of all of the many car rides Charles had given him over the years. In those moments just moving down the road, the conversations ranged from boring, to fascinating, and sometimes they were even insightful.

Purdue pulled up to the long driveway that led up to the property and parked. He would rather have a nice stroll up the drive. He brought the novel along with him, tucking under his arm as he walked. As he approached, he could see the house but his mind must have been playing tricks—it didn't look damaged at all.

It looked just as he imagined it in his memories and not at all like the pile of ashes and rubble he was expecting to see. He kept walking closer and the house still looked just as pristine as it always had. He expected his strange hallucination to dissipate at any moment, for his mind to snap back into reality—but the house continued to look exactly the same even as he stood right at the large front doors.

Purdue put his hand on the door and half-expected that his fingers would move seamlessly right through it like some sort of hologram. His mind was rearing with all kinds of possible explanations for what he was seeing and even feeling. There shouldn't have been nearly this much of his home left. There weren't even scorch marks from the inferno. The last time he'd seen the house, it was up in flames, a burning blaze against the darkness of the night sky.

Even in the time between, there was no way someone had already cleaned it up and then brought the house back into good condition. Even if they had, there was no way it could be so identical to how it used to be so quickly, and there would at least be some kind of visible damage from the fire. At the very least.

But there was nothing. Everything outside looked perfect.

He had to check inside. Surely there would be some evidence of the fire there, since that was where it originated from. He could still picture the halls engulfed in blankets of flames as Sasha led Purdue out of the hellfire as he was wheezing from smoke inhalation. That hadn't been any kind of trick. He'd felt the fire's heat—almost been melted by it.

Purdue cautiously opened up the front doors to the estate and stepped inside. It was exactly how he left it. Nothing was out of place. Even his books on various international architecture on the coffee table were in the exact right position as he would have expected. The shelves in his study were filled with the hundreds of books he bought over the years, not a single one missing or out of place. Those books all should have been easy prey for the fire that consumed the house—but apparently hadn't actually consumed it.

He was dumbstruck by it all. None of it made any sense for it all to still be there. He ran his fingertips along the walls and couldn't believe that he was able to touch the house that had been destroyed. Everything was exactly as it should be.

Purdue went from room to room, not skipping a single one as he made his way through the house. There were dozens of rooms to check but he made sure he inspected each one thoroughly and not a single one let him down. They all were precisely as they should be, as he still remembered them in his mind.

The house that the Order of the Black Sun stole from him was restored, like it had never been destroyed it all—but it had. That's what was baffling about the whole situation. That house should have at the very least had scorch marks all throughout it. But that was a serious fire that night that he remembered seeing tear down some of the roof and walls.

There should have been much more damage than there was.

Purdue took a seat in the comfiest chair; it rested beside the fireplace and was where Charles often spent some quiet time when he hadn't been running all over the place for his boss. It felt strange to be sitting in it, especially with Twenty Thousand Leagues Under the Sea in his hands. He could practically feel the spirit of Charles working through him.

That's when it occurred to him—as he sat there in Charles' seat by the fire with Charles' book in his grasp.

This was what Charles wanted.

As much as Purdue appreciated the role Charles played in stopping Julian Corvus and saving him, he knew the man well enough to know that he wouldn't usually have chosen to dive headfirst into battle. Charles would have definitely preferred a quiet night where he could read his book in peace.

He thought back to Charles' body on the altar and the book and wine beside him after the sacrifice had been performed. All Charles wanted was to be at home, reading his book, and sipping on his drink by the fireplace. He was a simple man sometimes with unexciting ambitions but he was loyal and responsible to a fault some times. He just needed a break here and there.

But he hardly ever did.

His wish was to be able to enjoy a quiet moment in his home reading his favorite book. That wish would have been impossible to grant with the house burned to the ground. Without probably even realizing it, Charles' dying wish had reconstructed the old estate to its former glory. This was just another part of his wish, and it had been fulfilled. Sure, Charles wouldn't be able to read by the fireplace again but Purdue still could and that was exactly what he intended to do.

Purdue knew he could always count on his late butler. Even in death, Charles was still surprising Purdue and helping provide for him. The house that had been set ablaze and destroyed had returned and Purdue felt at home again. Charles always used to make sure that Purdue was comfortable in his surroundings, and was still making sure that he was at ease.

Charles truly was a good friend, and a master butler.

There would be no way to replace him, even with the entire Order of the Black Sun now at his beck and call. Purdue got comfy and sat back in his seat. He opened to the first page of Twenty Thousand Leagues Under the Sea, turning a page that Charles had turned literally thousands and thousands of times during his own many readings of that book. Purdue started at the very first page and began his research. The first page struck him immediately:

The year 1866 was signalized by a remarkable incident, a mysterious and inexplicable phenomenon, which doubtless no one has yet forgotten.

Now Purdue could just take a breath and enjoy someone else's adventures of discovery.

It was what Charles would have wanted.

Now that he had the Order of the Black Sun on his side rather than as an enemy, the path ahead was impossible to predict. Even Mama May and all of her psychic wisdom probably would have struggled with seeing it.

But like Captain Nemo, David Purdue loved diving headfirst into the unknown.

EPILOGUE – THE ROCKING CHAIR

The rocking chair creaked and that creak moved its way through the peculiar house. It was a non-verbal message to the others in the house and a reminder about who was in charge. No matter where someone was in the house, the noises she usually made always found the proper ears that she wanted to hear what she had to say.

Her house was an odd one, especially compared to most others' her age. It was filled with historical trinkets that most people wouldn't even bother with. There was silverware from a shipwreck and even weaponry from a bygone era. A long barrel of a destroyed tank hung from her wall, protruding out toward another office, but a temporary fix.

Of course she had heard the whispers. That was all she ever seemed to hear. Most people were too afraid to speak at a normal volume around her, not wanting to concern an old bird like her with anything that she might not like. The truth was, it took a lot to upset her. It wasn't that she was frail and her body wasn't capable of getting energetic anymore, it was that there was very little in the world that actually surprised her anymore. Nearly ten decades was enough to make anyone jaded.

Her life was a long story but just a small footnote on the story of the world as a whole. Personal history was always so minute in comparison. Everyone always said that she was so wise and knew so much but the truth was that it had nothing to do with her first hand experiences. Most of her knowledge came from study. She had spent her decades pouring over every aspect of history, every little detail of every little event. Even when sitting in a room with the world's top historians, she could tell them things that they could never have hoped to remember.

"The Order of the Black Sun has changed management yet again," she said softly, mostly to herself. "Yes, I have heard those whispers. That violent little upstart did not last too long at all then, did he? Shameful. He made such a mess with everything and it was not even worth it in the end. I would have commended him if his plans came to fruition, as much as I disdain that pretentious club of theirs."

"And you have heard who has taken charge?"

Oddly, those whispers had never reached her ears. That was a rarity but she did love when it happened. It opened up the possibility that she would actually be surprised, but even then, she hardly ever was.

She imagined that in the fallout of Julian Corvus's removal, another one of those misguided fools would take his place. She had put her chips on the girl, Sasha, but that had been dashed by her untimely death. She would have said Vincent Moore but he was killed around the same time. Even the ruling council—some of whom she had long history with—had all been butchered by Julian Corvus. All of the good candidates had been brushed away and only Corvus' menagerie of sycophants had any hopes of rising. Perhaps that egotistical little Irishman, Galen Fitzgerald had finally clawed his way to the top of the heap—but a pathetic man like him would certainly not last long. He'd be gone even quicker than Julian Corvus.

"I have not," she admitted dryly, her mind starting to fill with anticipation. "Who is it?"

Hopefully this wouldn't be another predictable letdown.

"David Purdue."

There it was. The sweet sensation of legitimate surprise.

"David Purdue?" She asked, just to make sure she had even heard right. As good as her hearing was, she always had to check to make sure her old age wasn't catching up with her. "That could not be...no. He has long since been an enemy to the Order of the Black Sun, causing all kinds of trouble all over the world. Even when they thought they killed him, he remained steadfast in his ways. I, of course, knew of his survival, but I wasn't going to do the Black Sun any favors. David Purdue was their mess, and he is a messy one. The Wharf Man of the Jamaican coast lost his life in some gamble with David Purdue recently. From what I had heard, he was plotting to destroy the order single-handedly. I thought he was a fool."

"He may be, but yes, he is now the leader of the Order of the Black Sun. It's been confirmed."

"Interesting. To defeat his enemies, he supplanted them entirely. It is a bold move but he is, of course, a bold man. I wonder how the rest of the order will react to having to follow a man that they tried to kill so many times. Truly remarkable risk he is taking. But I would gladly take him over that Corvus fool. At least David Purdue respects the history. Perhaps this will be a positive thing for such a volatile group."

"What are we going to do about it?"

"For now, nothing," she said firmly. "We will wait and see what David Purdue has in store for the Order of the Black Sun. Perhaps he will surprise me again."

"And if he doesn't?"

The old woman's rocking chair squeaked

underneath her and her lips formed a wrinkled smile.

"Then we will show him the real history of the Order of the Black Sun."

END

Made in the USA
San Bernardino, CA
04 April 2020

66927550R00144